The Raven of Ruwi
and Other Stories from Oman

Middle East Literature in Translation
Michael Beard and Adnan Haydar, *Series Editors*

For a full list of titles in this series, visit
https://press.syr.edu/supressbook-series
/middle-east-literature-in-translation/.

The Raven of Ruwi

and Other Stories from Oman

HAMOUD SAUD

Translated from the Arabic by Zia Ahmed

Syracuse University Press

These stories were originally published in Arabic in غراب البنك ورائحة روي
(*Ghurāb al-bank wa raiḥat Ruwi*) (Beirut: Dar Soual, 2017),
أحلام معلقة على جسر وادي عدي (*Aḥlām mu'allaqa 'ala jisr Wadi Adai*)
(Beirut: Dar Soual, 2019), and أشجار الرماد وأعمى مراكش (*Ashjār al-ramād
wa a'mā Marrakesh*) (Tangier: Dar Agora, 2022). "The French Ship's Dog"
was originally published in Arabic in *Nizwa* magazine.

26 27 28 29 30 31   6 5 4 3 2 1

For a listing of books published and distributed by Syracuse University Press,
visit https://press.syr.edu.

ISBN: 9780815612018 (paperback)
9780815657637 (e-book)

Library of Congress Cataloging-in-Publication Data

Names: Sa'ūd, Ḥammūd author | Ahmed, Zia (Translator) translator
Title: The raven of Ruwi and other stories from Oman / Hamoud Saud ;
translated from the Arabic by Zia Ahmed.
Description: First edition. | Syracuse, New York : Syracuse
University Press, 2026. | Series: Middle East literature in translation
Identifiers: LCCN 2025042729 (print) | LCCN 2025042730 (ebook) |
ISBN 9780815612018 paperback | ISBN 9780815657637 ebook
Subjects: LCSH: Sa'ūd, Ḥammūd—Translations into English |
BISAC: FICTION / Short Stories (single author) | HISTORY /
Middle East / Arabian Peninsula | LCGFT: Short stories
Classification: LCC PJ7962.A9326 R38 2026 (print) | LCC PJ7962.A9326 (ebook)
LC record available at https://lccn.loc.gov/2025042729
LC ebook record available at https://lccn.loc.gov/2025042730

The authorized representative in the EU for product
safety and compliance is Mare Nostrum Group B.V.
Doelen 72, 4831 GR Breda, The Netherlands
gpsr@mare-nostrum.co.uk

for the margin, the marginals, and the marginalized

Contents

Map of Muscat, Oman, by Bushra Al Zuhaimi

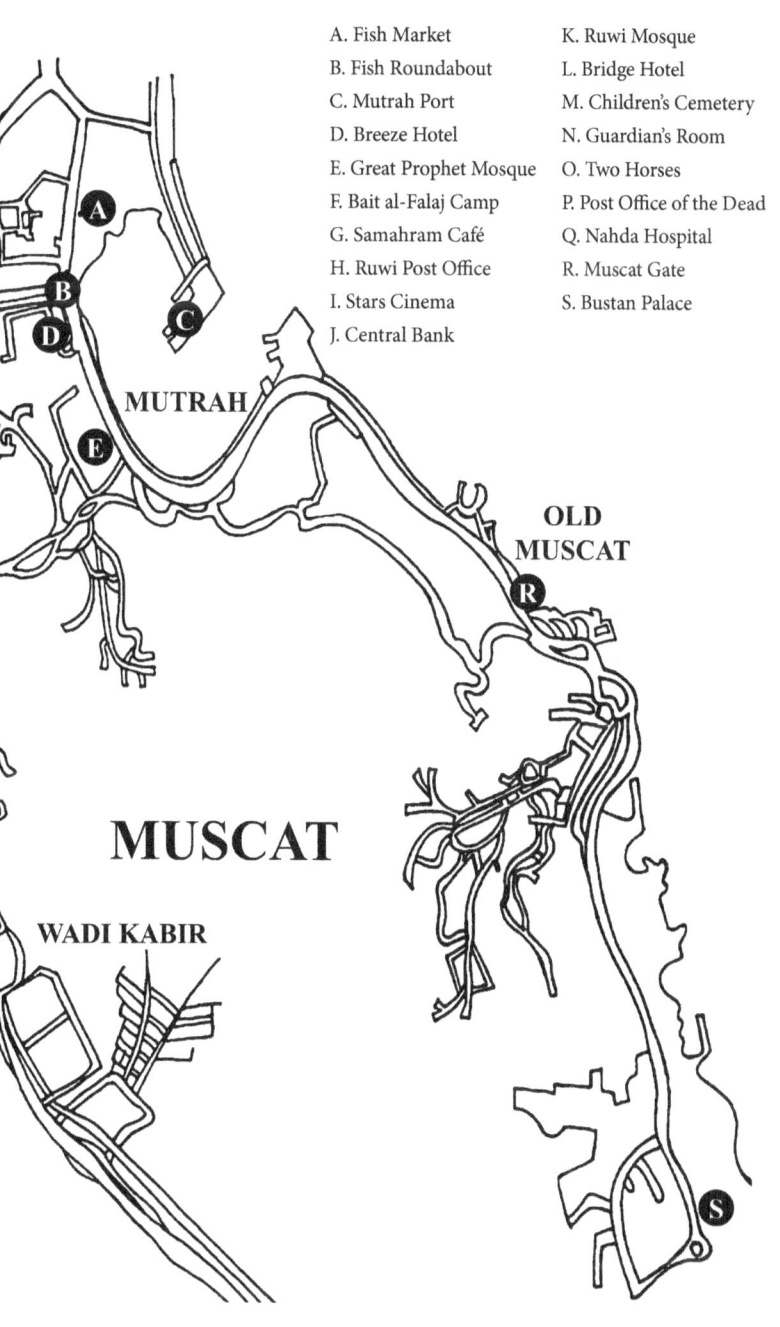

A. Fish Market
B. Fish Roundabout
C. Mutrah Port
D. Breeze Hotel
E. Great Prophet Mosque
F. Bait al-Falaj Camp
G. Samahram Café
H. Ruwi Post Office
I. Stars Cinema
J. Central Bank
K. Ruwi Mosque
L. Bridge Hotel
M. Children's Cemetery
N. Guardian's Room
O. Two Horses
P. Post Office of the Dead
Q. Nahda Hospital
R. Muscat Gate
S. Bustan Palace

MUTRAH

OLD
MUSCAT

MUSCAT

WADI KABIR

Foreword

We took a road trip together once, Hamoud Saud and I, during which he taught me the names of all the trees we passed on the way from the capital, Muscat, to the Sultanate of Oman's Al Sharqiya region. He explained the difference between a *samura* tree and a *sidra*, and how to distinguish between the *ṭalḥ* and *sanṭ*—both from the same acacia family—that were scattered, un-pruned, on either side of the highway. He spoke about the wadi and its stones, the sand and its dunes, giving life to stones and plants with his words. When mountain shepherds sang the hymns of eternity, he joined in and became the voice. When mesmerizing sand formations were tinted by the setting sun, he merged with the eternal golden hues.

Hamoud Saud—who, in his prose, seems immersed in the urban, represented by Muscat and its rapid, astonishing transformations—is also deeply connected with nature, with *falaj* and tree, sand and sea, especially its spiritual horizons and its representations of elevating the human within us.

Muscat, the metropolis, and its surroundings—Mutrah, Qurayyat, Al Amerat, Khuwair—dominate Hamoud Saud's narrative world. But, for him, a place is not merely the setting for a written text, but its main character—not static, but dynamic, changing, following the developments and setbacks that befall the city, and being affected by them in turn.

In this context—of place dominating narrative—Hamoud Saud is preoccupied with describing the lives of people of diverse origins, races, languages, and religions, all enclosed within the space of Muscat. These people create the place, give it its character, and at times they are the ones who rip the spirit out of the place, stripping it of human qualities. It's as if the city in these stories endows human lives with their worth, limits the scope of their movement, and determines their status in a social hierarchy created by people, who are then subjugated by it.

Throughout its long history, Omani literature has primarily celebrated poetry, whose affluence has continued unabated for centuries, both in Oman itself and in regions formerly under its influence in East Africa, such as Zanzibar, where the first Arabic-language Omani newspaper was published in 1911. As a result, short-story collections were not published in Oman until the early 1980s, a period when the names of Omani writers were limited and their literary experiments still in the early stages of artistic maturity. Omani short fiction did not begin to flourish and mature until the generation preceding Hamoud Saud's, then his own. The Omani writer turned to his environment, drawing stories from it, making cities and villages the space in which narrative events unfold, and using their people for characters that reflected the concerns of contemporary Omanis, with their customs and traditions as the framework for his stories and narrative worlds.

Born in 1982, in the city of Samail, Hamoud Saud is unique among these writers for making the urban Omani setting—specifically, Muscat—the protagonist of his narrative texts. He writes about *place*, preoccupied with all its manifestations and transformations, as if place is what gives the people of his stories their identity, fulfilling their hopes or destroying their dreams. From these stories we sense that the writer's representation of reality is the vision of a seer, which transforms a songbird into a symbol, a tree into a tale, a country into breath and essence, and a guardian into a knowing dreamer bearing symbols and possibilities for interpretation. No wonder, then, that his book *Dreams Suspended on Wadi Adai Bridge* won the award for Best Omani Publication from the Omani Writers Association in 2019. His sensitivity and delicacy in writing are remarkable, with narrative worlds that blend the imaginary with the realistic, the dreamlike with the symbolic, humanizing inanimate objects. These translated stories are selected from *Dreams Suspended on Wadi Adai Bridge*, *The Bank Raven and the Scent of Ruwi* (2017), and *Trees of Ash and the Blind Man of Marrakesh* (2022), which are among the five books he published between 2013 and 2022.

Perhaps this exquisite translation by writer and translator Zia Ahmed opens up horizons for savoring the worlds of Hamoud Saud, drawing attention to his narrative eye, which observes the braids of a cheerful Indian girl, the lumbering gait of an Egyptian woman, and the tree of an Omani passerby in front of the Central Bank—the eye that follows the shifting of symbols on roundabouts, the transformation of shops into malls, the relocation of horse statues from place to place. In his stories, we read the political depth of human affairs, for there is a story hidden within each story, which this collection is an invitation to examine, and to open up to the richness of Omani literature as a whole.

Jokha Alharthi
Muscat, Oman
Translated by Zia Ahmed

Translator's Introduction

Hamoud Saud is a teller—qās, in Arabic—of short stories, memoirish vignettes, prose poems, and other strange
sketches that defy easy categorization. Geography, history,
and memory link the narrative texts (as one of his books
describes its contents) that you hold in your hands, each set
in a neighborhood of the Omani capital, Muscat. The fab-
ulistic, often spiritual work of this unconventional writer
from a country on the geographic and theological margins
of the Arab world reflects his sense of a life lived in intel-
lectual exile. As he puts it in "The Blood of Solitude":

> Writing that eludes me, fleeing like a mountain
> goat from the cage of paper and screen; writing that
> burrows behind thresholds, that emerges from the
> depths of simple thoughts; writing that is concealed
> or revealed by language, or flows from the margins or
> shadows; writing that probes the depths of pain and
> joy; writing that is dream, reality, and imagination . . .
> that's the writing I think of, always.

Once a proud maritime empire that stretched from
the East African coast to parts of modern-day Pakistan,

Oman increasingly came under British influence in the nineteenth century, partly owing to imperial anxieties about the jewel in the crown, India. Not surprisingly, Britons and South Asians appear often in Hamoud's writing: the former as invaders who "latch on to the country's jugular and drink its blood" in the nightmarish "Pirates of Wadi Adai," and the latter as modern Oman's largest guest-worker community, whose cultural and culinary influences some regard with wariness. Ruwi, the Muscat neighborhood that serves as the setting for the eponymous title story, isn't Chennai, but you can smell the spices of India wafting from its side streets and restaurants, as the narrator of "The Raven of Ruwi" gently complains.

The discovery of oil brought stunningly swift modernity to Oman, which in 1970 had (perhaps apocryphally) three miles of paved roads, three schools, and three clinics—a past within living memory that's unfathomable to the outsider today, amid multilane highways, gleaming malls, and immaculate public infrastructure. Not everyone cherishes a "cruel and deformed modernity" that makes people forget the mud houses of their villages and neglect their memories, as we find in "Marginalizing the Narrative, Narrating the Marginal." Nostalgia, for lost childhood and a simpler past, is a defining aspect of the sensitive Omani psyche, heartbreakingly endured by the tragic titular character of "The Guardian of Muscat," who, while recalling the scent of lemons from faraway villages, sees "nothing but asphalt and lights, a life without life."

This, then, is what rapid modernization has wrought in Hamoud's hometown, seen through the eyes of his "sad donkey of Muscat": a place of "exile and alienation, a stranger to itself," where children plant their dreams but one that devours the children and their dreams. *Muscat* means "place of falling" in Arabic, we learn from "Who Stole Muscat's Noses?" "Things fall in this city every morning: dreams fall, words fall from newspapers, delusional people fall into the traps of light, nostalgia falls upon its ancient paths." Here, city dwellers "gather by the sea to try to catch the fish of an idyllic past, but instead the whale of a predatory present assails them, devouring their joy, their voices, their memories, so that, ultimately, they fall victim to the maw of a ravenous future."

Oman's history reverberates through Hamoud's writing, including murmurs of Ibadism, the moderate Islamic sect whose gentle ethos of tolerance and coexistence permeates Omani society. But it wasn't always so. Ibadi imams once ruled a muscular theocracy in inner Oman, separated from the seafaring sultanate by stony mountains that guarded coastal Muscat from "white-turbaned dreams." Then there was the Dhofar War of the 1960s and '70s, a Marxist insurgency that turned the country into "a boiling cauldron of heat and anxiety," forcing the desperate protagonist of "The Raven of Ruwi" to enlist, drawing him south, toward the war.

But history, memory, and geography are mere muses for Hamoud's Sufi sensibility, whose ultimate subject is the inner life, revealed through deceptively simple themes: trees, Muscat landmarks, and a profound yearning for childhood. This is his parting gift—a guide for how to lead a spiritual life:

So don't follow the sun of the generals or the lights of illusion. Like a Sufi, you must listen to what the shadows say. Watch the child's wonder in a mirror, contemplate the waitress's sadness at a café or in a poem. Be like a blind man leading the flock of his stories in the mirrors of time.

Z. A.

December 2024

McLean, Virginia

The Raven of Ruwi
and Other Stories from Oman

The Raven of Ruwi

Are you worried?

What worries you?

We must fill this blank page with sounds, stories, smells, breaks, and footnotes to complete the forest of narrative. Dear narrator, don't worry about all the critical theories that Arab academics pursue like famished camels, whose number exceeds the grains of sand in the Empty Quarter. Let's go together to the Muscat neighborhood of Ruwi; let's explore the place, its shadows, sounds, and streets, the smells of its passersby, and the trees overlooking its balconies. Let's leave the literary fanatics in their ivory towers. First off, my narrator friend, let me tell you: Ruwi isn't Chennai, for it doesn't resemble any Indian city. Ruwi resembles itself, even though its smells, trees, thresholds, alleyways, and musical languages contradict the previous statement. The Indian girls walking to the cinema in their finery will say to you: Ruwi was our childhood. Indian music will emanate from the balconies overlooking Ruwi's streets. The scents will whisper to you that you're in Ruwi. Even the

1

flower-covered decks of some apartments will tell you that you're in Ruwi.

You'll smell the spices of India wafting from the side streets and humble restaurants, even if you have a head cold. The morning song of the street cleaner, hummed as he sweeps away the night's fatigue and the languor of pedestrians, tells you that you're in Ruwi. Ruwi the stranger, estranged from itself. Ruwi of the doves, of balconies and conversations, saturated with stories, with forgetfulness and the joy of passersby.

1

Samahram Café crouches like a hungry frog below the Bait al-Hafa hotel. Let's rest here for a little while before the ships of the story depart for distant shores. You're not in Salalah,[1] but in Ruwi of Indian scents. What do Ruwi, India, and Salalah have in common?

I remember a story Abdullah Habib told me about an Indian couple he met in Britain.[2] After they'd broken the ice, the man said he'd fought in the Dhofar War.

Don't worry, narrator, either about the war or about the story of the Indian man in Britain. Let's drink our coffee, quickly or slowly, it doesn't matter, for the ships haven't yet set sail. Let's contemplate the blue dome of Ruwi Mosque, which contrasts the blue of the sky and the flocks of doves and the taxi drivers and the seekers of jobs, hope, and love. If you're hungry, the Haikal restaurant is near the mosque. Don't blame me after you've eaten an Indian meal there with enough chili to burn through all of Ruwi, not just your stomach.

From the café's rose-decorated balcony, you can see the travel agencies across the street. Music will descend upon you from the café's ceiling, chosen for you by the mood of the Filipina waitress. You'll see Asian workers and Arab families entering and leaving the travel agencies, plane tickets in their hands, tears and songs in their hearts.

Trees and lampposts stand in front of the travel agencies, as if the trees are guarding the tickets and tears of the travelers, while the lampposts are gallows for their years of exile. The trees neither travel nor dream of plane tickets, but they open their hearts to Ruwi's doves and the shadows on the roads and the tired bodies of the workers in the afternoon, doves that color Ruwi's sky and courtyards and balconies with joy. The trees dig their roots into the soil, holding tight to Ruwi's origins.

2

An Indian song plays on the screen, the screen hangs on a colorless wall without history, the wall is in a tavern, the tavern is in Ruwi, and Ruwi supports the windows of the story. In the old Ruwi tavern, an elderly Indian man told me about his great-great-grandfather who'd fought in the 1820 military campaign in Jalan Bani Bu Ali under a British general. His ancestor had died, along with many Indians led by the general.

Then, he cursed the British with all of India's curses in all its languages. The screen fell silent, the wall collapsed, the tavern shut down, and the elderly Indian man moved away from Ruwi. Only the story remained, silently, in Ruwi, and the windows of the story remained open.

3

Let's leave war, history, and the British, my narrator friend. Let's walk past the signs for the Ministry of Sports and head east. On your left, you'll see people leaving church, with forests of colors and the scents of prayers, sins, and dried tears. If you turn to the right, a harsh mountain range will slap you in the face. Neither trees nor ideas, not even demon heads, grow there. Behind these mountains sleeps the Wadi Kabir industrial area, with a graveyard for cars, and stories of asphalt death and the clash of iron with modernity. These are the mountains that guard Ruwi and Mutrah from seventeenth-century pirates and invasions from inner Oman, and from white-turbaned dreams.

Let's go this evening and listen to the voices of people and roads, and then let's visit the commercial district, with the post office at its center. Before the post office stands the communications tower that some Omanis call Qaraqir Wald Humaidan. Don't ask me who he is, inquisitive narrator, because I don't know. Perhaps he's a sheikh or a fishmonger or a taxi driver. Also before the post office is a lonely *sharīsh* tree, guarding the Bait al-Falaj military camp. The *sharīsh* doesn't drink from the country's *falaj* or from the story's source.[3] On the tree sleeps a raven from the Empty Quarter, who's headed for the Indian Ocean, carrying messages from the mountains and the desert, tales of the ancestors kneaded with blood, betrayal, and dreams. The post office itself is obscured by *sharīsh* and tamarind trees. Perhaps these are the only trees capable of delivering our dreams, poems, and tears to the heavens. Letters no longer come here.

The guard tells me, "I used to open mailboxes for lovers and expatriates, but now I only guard these walls, water the trees every morning, and watch the Indian women going to their jobs, dreams, church, and cinema. I stare at the balconies and the clothes hanging from them."

Only the tree by the entrance of the post office realizes that letters no longer reach the mother because she's now in the cemetery.

They don't reach the lover because he went blind.

They don't reach the soldier because now he has no legs and no heart.

Nor the prisoner because he has become numb.

4

You may sleep, dear narrator, in the shade near the Bait al-Falaj military camp. You could also bathe in the eponymous *falaj* or fish in it for stories while I arrange a curious tale in my head, following the silent one that escaped from the tavern.

Here I am, standing near the café by the post office. I see a man lighting his pipe in the summer of 1972, more specifically the afternoon of July 15. Muscat is a boiling cauldron of heat and anxiety because of the war. I see the man resting under a shady *ghāf* tree. The tree stands where the Stars Cinema came up years later. Back then, there was neither cinema nor stars, just war and blood and armies. Immigrants in exile drew their hunger and alienation on the walls of their narrow, miserable rooms. It was an anxious time.

The man resting under the *ghāf* tree had returned a month earlier from exile in the Persian Gulf after the newspapers and white men's embassies told him he must go back to plant trees of renaissance and restore the memory of a country burdened by war, drought, and fear.

The night before, he'd slept in Wadi Adai, alone, staring at the sky of his dreams and the stars of his country, listening to the night hiss. Under a lonely mountain, he was shrouded in dreams, fear, and hunger. In the barren forest of Muscat, he'd been searching for a job. I see him watching the white and red soldiers entering the Bait al-Falaj camp with their stars, swords, and anger. The man said to himself, "Neither is the house ours, nor will the *falaj* irrigate the country."

Here I see him, that afternoon, approaching the gate guarded by soldiers and rifles. He said to them, "I want a job."

I see him now, the man who'd been standing under the tree in the place of Stars Cinema, in a military transport truck, carrying clothes in a black bag, heading south, toward the war.

The narrator, who was sleeping under the tree after bathing in the camp's *falaj* and fishing for stories, started shaking my hand and shouting at me, "Hey, you, haunted by your wounded and forgotten history—it's 2015, not 1972. I'll order you a coffee from the post office café."

Section Outside the Text

The man riding the troop carrier recounted a missing part of the story forty-three years later, painstakingly excavating the words from his memory:

"We left Bait al-Falaj and went to Rustaq. The people of Rustaq were really brave. Every day there was a mine; every day there was an operation. The army camped at Al Hazm. The British went completely insane. One year the rebels came from Al Batinah at night in a car loaded with weapons, with Dubai and Kuwait plates. One of them attacked the checkpoint and destroyed the wireless. They killed him, and the rest fled, five of them, I think. We were resting in the camp. Everyone was confused: the soldiers, the British, the world. All night long, the army searched the villages and surrounding wilderness. They were finally caught and taken back to Bait al-Falaj, where the intelligence services had a camp. The British were ruthless and didn't show mercy, not to anyone."

5

Dear narrator, you can sit at the small café near the Central Bank in Ruwi any evening you like, and you can observe things, people, cars, cats, and doves on the sidewalks from any angle you like. You can see the traffic policeman's hand writing letters and numbers.

Working at the tiny café you see six Indians of the same family from Hyderabad. Of course, in this slight chill, you can order *karak* for one hundred *baisas*,[4] or black *qahwa* if you are from the Socialist Party of Coffee.

You have to raise your sight and foresight a little to see, on the café's opposite side, an Indian music school for boys and girls. At the entrance, you'll see an Indian teenager trying to memorize a poem by Tagore, her phone playing a song by Kareena Kapoor.

An Indian woman's gold-covered hand will open her BMW's back door to let out her daughter, guitar on her back and love songs in her heart. The daughter will plant a quick kiss on her fortysomething mother's cheek before she enters the school.

Sit down for a bit, dear narrator. Finish your cup of coffee. At five o'clock, the bank's employees will leave. If you look at them emerging from the jungle of money, business, and dreams, you'll see only fatigue and exhaustion.

You must relax your head, narrator. Try to raise it to the sky. Naturally, Ruwi's sky won't rain gold despite all these banks, but it'll definitely rain Indian music. You'll see doves swimming in the sky above Ruwi and Darsait. The doves land on the balconies and sidewalks, seeking sustenance for the long night ahead.

The Indian girls will walk by you, languid narrator. You ponder the forests of colors in their clothes and listen to the music of their language. The girls crossing the street to the cinema will watch on the screen with astonishment the narrator sitting alone in a café. The narrator, who waits at five thirty in the evening to see the Indian couple employed at the currency exchange, will see the wife walking alone past the Central Bank, her head bowed, counting her steps and memories. The narrator will know from the tears falling on the asphalt that her husband has departed this country and his life.

6

I saw them dead: generals, poets, fishermen, soldiers without guns, revolutionaries who left their revolution in history books, shepherds without mountains, students without a national anthem, women without motherhood, workers without dreams. I saw them enter the Bait al-Falaj tavern this evening.

The narrator said to me, "How do you see, when you left your eyes behind at the tree?"

"I saw the tears and disappointment, and that's enough for me."

7

That evening, I was sitting in a secluded café overlooking the street. A woman was crossing over to the other side. I was contemplating the forests of colors crossing the black street.

The moment the woman finished crossing the street, the raven from the Empty Quarter atop the Central Bank cawed, then landed on the bank's gate. An Indian teenager took out her pink phone. Before she could touch the screen with her index finger, the raven flew away, coming to rest on top of the post office to deliver messages to its friends and the dead bank guard.

8

At five in the evening, the Egyptian woman who lives alone in a one-bedroom apartment near Stars Cinema will emerge, holding a phone to her ear. Don't ask me, inquisitive narrator, how I knew she was Egyptian and that she lives near the cinema. First, you mustn't cut the frayed thread of narrative in this text, because I have nothing to which I can connect the story when it's interrupted. Second, when I was walking past the row of banks each evening to soothe my soul from the vipers of work and the wolves of routine, you were asleep and let the story deviate.

For half a year, the thirtysomething Egyptian woman has walked here every day. I don't know the reason for her daily commitment to walking. Is she a doctor or a gym instructor?

Through her daily calls and brisk walk, I learned that her father was in prison because of the events of June 30. Inquisitive narrator, permit me to clarify to you the narrative that was interrupted and the story's thread that was cut off because you were napping under the Bait al-Falaj tree. On the sixth of April, during her usual long call with her mother—who, by the way, is in Cairo Hospital, at the end of Salah Salem Street, because she has cancer—the woman said:

"Don't cry, Mama. You're so sick, why worry yourself more by crying?"

"Father will be free soon. I sent money to the lawyer, and he assured me."

"He told me, literally, one to three months, and he'll be out."

"By the way, Mama, I'll go on vacation with you over the Eid holidays."

This Cairene woman in her thirties continues her daily rituals: a long call, after which she drinks from the small bottle she holds in her hand. In the distance, close to the row of banks, her quick steps cut through time and anxiety and the shade of palm trees standing guard over the palace.

After she's finished with her daily ritual, she'll get in her small red car in the parking lot of Alizz Islamic Bank. From the car window, Hany Shaker's voice will pierce the Ruwi evening.

We come into the world not knowing why, nor where
    we go, nor what we want.
On paths drawn for our steps we walk, through the
    loneliness of our nights.
One day makes us happy, another wounds us, and we
    don't know why.

9

The raven flying over the Central Bank each evening at six thirty must convey its messages without the symbolism of the murderer and the murdered and their sins, without the teachings of the first teacher. Nobody here pays attention to the first teacher, or to the dying wishes of the murdered. This country doesn't heed the symbolism of a raven flying over the Central Bank each evening, noticed only by the imagination of a delusional and inquisitive narrator. The country is preoccupied with its hunger and its oil. The oil will dry up, and the dreams of the country's children will dry up with it.

I'm not a prophet to translate the language of birds for you. I don't have time to explain what the raven said or what its messages conveyed atop the building of your cash deposits and the reservoir of your livelihoods. When the raven flies by with its symbolism and timing (half past six in the evening), I'm busy at the post office café, reading the letters of the dead and the martyrs and the women wading through their loss and eternal absence. I look at two Indian teenagers crossing the street to Stars Cinema. I study an apartment balcony, with trees and songs and an Indian lady trying to capture Ruwi's setting sun through the lens of her iPhone.

You must listen carefully to the messages of the raven perched on the Central Bank's flagpole. You must stop the disaster.

10

There's a lonely raven perched above the Central Bank in Ruwi's commercial district at six thirty every evening.

It recites the odes of the ancestors.

It sings for Azzan bin Qais.[5]

It foretells famine and hunger.

It paints the footpaths with dreams.

It says to the country, be less concerned with metaphor.

It says to the expanse, be a song and a wound.

11

At six thirty this evening, the raven from the Empty Quarter won't fly over the Central Bank in Ruwi's commercial district, because for years it has preached its commandments and shouted in the face of disaster, saying to the country and its people what the poet says to the poem, what the bullet says to the dead man, what the tree says to the Sufi's reed flute, what the mountains whisper to the shepherds and the drought. But the country and its people accused the raven of madness, jealousy, and treason.

An octogenarian Indian woman told me about the raven from the Empty Quarter, which preached its commandments and said to the country, "Be less dry than exile." On the afternoon of the fifteenth of July—more precisely when the sun was at its zenith—the raven searched for an end worthy of its language and existential alienation, and its abandoned and forgotten commandments. It was thinking about a bullet from the Bait al-Falaj camp, but instead it chose the tires of a speeding woman's car to end its commandments and prayers.

12

Again, at six thirty in the evening, also in Ruwi's business district, I see Patrick Süskind, the German author of *Perfume*, exiting the cinema, carrying nostalgic letters and yellowing notebooks. He's walking to the post office, but stops at the gate of the Central Bank fortified by walls, cameras, imposing doors, and the dreams of the poor. He stands under a tree near the gate. The guard is asleep.

Süskind lifts his head and sees a raven's nest. He looks at the nest, the raven, the tree, and the bank.

He opens a yellow notebook and scribbles some notes. He writes several lines on the trunk of the palm tree by the bank gate. He places a sheet of paper on the sleeping guard's chest, then resumes his walk to the post office.

He sends a message to his murderer, and to a dove sleeping above the door of a small hotel room on the outskirts of Paris.

Then he goes to the Bait al-Falaj tavern to read his scribblings about invaders and pirates, murderers and mountain shepherds, soldiers robbed of feeling by war, women without memory, and poets without tongues.

I see Süskind return once again, this time to sleep under the tree on which the raven from the Empty Quarter slept, after he'd written quick notes about the tavern wall and the hand of the African waitress.

13

Let's leave the raven preaching its commandments to which no one pays heed. Let's listen instead to the barking of a dog near the well of the Central Bank, the dog of an Indian family from Kerala. The Indian family was displaced by the financial crisis that the country is experiencing. In a garden near the commercial district grows a shady *sidra* tree. Under the *sidra* passes a stream that springs from the mountains near Wadi Kabir. The dog stretches its body under the tree's shade. Five crows land near it. It barks and they fly off. It shakes its head, heavy with weariness, boredom, and despair. The crows return;

it barks again. Between the game of shade, dog, and crows, the narrator spends his afternoon close to the *sidra* tree. At five in the evening, a teenage Indian girl walks past the dog, who will sleep tonight in one of the apartments near the commercial district. Only the narrator remains homeless in his country that he loves so much.

14

At ten in the evening, I left the newspaper office with my bank card and text-message reminders to buy milk and bread for the morning. As I walked out to the street, I remembered the lethargic narrator who slept at his desk, close to the story. I turned to him. When I turned back, I heard the screeching tires of a car . . .

A car pouncing on a body.

I see a head roll like an airless ball over the street and come to rest on the Central Bank's wall. Just as a man got out of his car to inspect the body drowning in blood, the raven from the Empty Quarter descended from the Central Bank's flagpole, walked ten steps, and pecked at the body. It took a small piece of the heart and flew off, landing back on the flagpole. A few drops of blood dripped from its beak. Two fell on the hand of the Indian teenager who'd meant to photograph the raven. Süskind passed the body without looking at it or making any notes. The Egyptian woman also crossed the street, still comforting her mother. Likewise, the bank guard didn't concern himself with the body or the head that stained the wall. He continued to listen to a song his wife had sent him as a birthday gift. Even the man who stood under the tree in the summer of 1972, before he went south to the war, didn't pay any attention to the body, although they'd shared kinship, blood, and stories.

The man who'd fled the old Ruwi tavern after the television screen went dark also walked past the corpse and didn't turn around.

The body is alone, its head on the Central Bank's wall. The guard has fallen asleep again. The raven is enjoying the scene as if it were the last warrior standing after a historic battle.

Everyone ignored the body. The narrator slept at his desk, guarding the story from thieves and informants. The text was never published. Ruwi's scents won't waft, and the raven won't come down.

These are the fingers of a man without memory, sitting in a café across from the bank. The fingers made some notes before the café closed.

On a sheet of paper that he requested from the waiter, the man in the café, who'd witnessed the full details of the death, wrote: "Perhaps it was the Indian intelligence agency that orchestrated the man's death. Perhaps it was the agents of the raven from the Empty Quarter. Or perhaps a stray bullet from the Bait al-Falaj military camp fired in 1972 settled in the heart of this man who only wanted to buy bread and milk for his children."

15

At midnight, when Ruwi's bars, cafés, and movie theaters were packed, a nightmare assailed the narrator guarding the story on his computer screen. In the nightmare, the narrator saw the man who'd walked the streets of Ruwi with him in the story. He saw him, naked and headless, at the gate of the Bait al-Falaj camp. The soldiers guarding the camp stood alert with their machine guns and bullets. With hand gestures, he preached to them the commandments of his childhood. The soldiers were terrified. They didn't understand him and fired a barrage of bullets at his chest.

The narrator arose, terrified from the story, and backed away from the screen. The newspaper office door was shut. He waited a while until the editor went out to the parking lot to smoke. Then, still shaken by his nightmare, he sneaked out behind the editor.

Walking past the Central Bank, he was shocked at the sight of the head. He turned to his right and saw the body lying near a lamppost, stained with blood and forgetfulness. He lifted the body to his back, and then walked slowly between the tall buildings. Embassy flags fluttered as Indian songs and smells emanated from the balconies.

After crossing a little stream, he lowered the body to the ground, bathed it, and scattered some *sidra* leaves on it. Again, he carried the body. The bus station was closed. A waiter was locking up his restaurant for the night. Inside the Nightingale Café, he saw customers arguing over the result of a game. A taxi driver listened sadly to a song on the radio. He walked a little, and then put the body down in the courtyard of Ruwi Mosque. Two Indian men stood with him to pray over the body. He walked again toward Ruwi's roundabout.

At the very center of the roundabout, at a quarter past one, the narrator dug a grave for the man who'd accompanied him in the story. He placed the body in the hole and covered it with dirt, roses, and some *sharīsh* branches and *sidra* leaves. As he buried the body, he heard a song playing from an apartment balcony above the commercial center. He didn't place a headstone on the grave. Afterward, he walked some ways to the Bait al-Hafa hotel, entered Samahram Café, washed his hands and face, and ordered himself a coffee.

He began to cry.

Marginalizing the Narrative, Narrating the Marginal

I sway between sleep and consciousness, between waking up to tend the flock of my disappointments and staring at the world's grayish-white illusions.

Five in the morning.

Six . . .

Eight . . .

I think about the characters that refused to come to life on paper. I think about a concept of time that's been worrying me for ages, time's cruel ability to spontaneously sweep things away to their ends. I think about endings open to the possibility of surprise and disappointment. I think about many things, jumbled and ambiguous, some exceedingly peripheral, others that precipitated in my memory months or years ago. I think about the ability of human memory to store images, events, details, and smells, and about the exact moment in which we recall an idea.

I see a yellow piece of paper stuck to the back of the door. I open the door and the window, turn over the paper, close the door and half the window, and turn on the gas to boil water. I stare at the morning steam wafting through the kitchen window overlooking a huge *sharīsh* tree.

> Stuff from the wholesale store
> Fish / fruit / juice for Firas
> Repair kitchen faucet
> Car AC / Wadi Kabir

I drag myself over to the window and open it again. The water is boiling. It's insanely hot outside. What would Ibn Battuta say if he lived for just a month in Al Amerat?

The shadow of the *sharīsh* dances on the wall and window. In the shadow's dance, I sense the tree's joy in the morning, the sun, and life. I see the scents and sounds of childhood in the dancing shadow. I see women going to their dreams. I see them alone in mud houses, and I hear their songs as they tend to their flocks. In the dancing shadow, I also see anxiety, boredom, and things left unfinished.

s

Driving through the Madinat al-Nahda neighborhood, I see in the rearview mirror the richly hued but barren Al Tayeen mountains, desolate springs, and a sad donkey going about its day. Cement boxes sprout suddenly. How quickly human beings crowd into these boxes created by a cruel and deformed modernity! We've forgotten the mud houses of our villages and neglected our memories. In time, crueler, more tortured, lost, and broken creatures will emerge from these cement forests, creatures who abandoned the earth, light, shadows, and the scents of trees, their souls imprisoned in deadly cages of concrete. How ugly you are, cement, a cancer eating away at our humanity, our innocence, and the spontaneity of our feelings.

I drive by a farm, also surrounded by cement.

s

Near the police station, a lone eagle perches at the center of Al Hajar roundabout, which takes you to Qurayyat and eastern Oman. The eagle, which the municipality installed on a roundabout atop a small hill guarded by three palm trees, is attempting to fly away to the Bawshar mountains. Every time I drive by this roundabout, I see the lonely eagle yearning for sky, flight, and freedom. My boy raises his little finger and shouts: "Daddy, eeeeeagle!"

> Alone, like the eagle of Al Hajar roundabout,
> One wing guiding passersby to their east,
> While the other directs the fearful to the police,
> As it stares at the shadow of a tree.

You see an eagle frozen in place for years, a roundabout that leads you to eastern Oman, and a police station guarding passersby and the lone eagle. In the evening, some birds land on the eagle's head and wings. What pain and humiliation the poor eagle must feel, trapped by the municipality in the middle of a roundabout. I think it resembles an Arab ruler overthrown by the masses in his old age.

After that, you'll cross the Antelope Wilderness roundabout. Cement forests consumed the wilderness, forcing the antelope to flee to other freer and more iso-lated locations. But the name people gave to this round-about remained.

You look up and see the mountains that surround Al Amerat, overrun by cement forests. The mountain streams, acacia, and other desert trees have vanished, and human memory has vanished with them. Land specula-tors play their games of greed, raiding the dreams of the poor, who offer their necks to the knives of the repugnant capitalist banks.

At the last roundabout, heading toward Wadi Adai, you see two horses the municipality relocated from the garden of the posh Bustan Palace hotel, pulling a black iron cannon under the hellish Al Amerat sun. The two don't look like warhorses, pack animals, royal steeds, mountain stallions, or Trojan horses. I don't know what the person who moved these poor animals wanted to tell us by forcing them to drag a cannon aimed at the eastern mountains. What idea did he wish to convey by placing two horses under this infernal sun? The time of horse-drawn cannons came to an end centuries ago, but the time of Al Amerat is eternal.

Why do I burden things with more than what words, narrative, and reality can bear? Perhaps the Bustan Pal-ace officials thought the two horses in their garden were incompatible with the grandeur of the place, the sea, mo-dernity, and capitalism, so they gifted them to the mu-nicipality. The municipality exiled the poor animals here to roast in the afternoon heat, and abandoned another in front of its headquarters to guard against boredom and oblivion.

The two horses were comfortable in the Bustan Palace's garden. True, they couldn't graze on the green grass, but at least they could enjoy the smell of the sea, the sounds of music from the hotel lobby and windows, and the scents of bodies relaxing in the garden. Here are the two horses, flung by time and an unknown municipality employee onto the roundabout, pulling a heavy iron cannon as if they were in a colonial war, alone and seared by Al Amerat's scorching sun and the looks of passersby. The two guard the cemetery now. Perhaps the narrator's imagination will make a hasty journal entry: The cemetery's dead children were bored at night, so they led the horses to a pasture. Or they raced them toward the mountains. Perhaps the dead children would fight over who would take a horse to the *falaj* to quench its eternal thirst.

You leave Al Amerat and its imaginary horses, famished eagles, and cement forests.

You contemplate the myths of Wadi Adai, the legends of its mountains, and the magic of its colors, how they shimmer and mingle with each other. The solitude of the place tempts passersby to examine its exotic shape and structure. Who knows, perhaps Noah's ark passed through here after the flood on its way to the Empty Quarter, carrying the seeds of humanity free of evil. But evil will sprout as long as there is life. Noah's ark will pass through the narrator's imagination and the flood to cross

Wadi Adai, carrying animals and fear to a desert that protects them from water's wrath.

By the foot of the valley you see shepherds, shrouded in their mountains, shadows, solitude, and palm trees killed by drought and absence.

At the end of Wadi Adai, you'll see Nahda Hospital, which floods often. Recently, people have begun to joke about when it'll flood next, technology enabling their wisecracks to spread far and wide as memes on phone screens.

s

Just after the entrance to Wadi Kabir lies a forlorn car cemetery, bearing witness to the blood of souls who departed life because of iron. Treacherous, sharp, painful, maker of orphans: iron carries us to our dreams, deaths, and disappointments.

A roundabout once stood here, lofty and alone, home to flocks of pigeons. Then, the government removed the roundabout and built a bridge in the place of birds and grass, a bridge that didn't connect memory to place, but rather severed the arteries of the place's memory.

Ten years ago, in this iron cemetery, my father told me: "In the seventies, this place was a complete wilderness, without a single building. People from distant villages would camp here for days, even weeks."

Suddenly, the cars came and their death came with them. This cemetery came into being, what we now call the Wadi Kabir industrial area. Just as there are Omani villages that bury their dead according to tribe, here, too, each car tribe has its reserved section: this one for Toyota, that for Lexus, and over there for Nissan. Sometimes, we resemble murderers in many aspects.

The Pakistani mechanic lowers his hands into the car's lungs to clean its windpipes and ease its breathing in the blazing Omani summer that burns trees and stones alike. I start a casual conversation. He tells me about his years in this cemetery. He talks about his family, Karachi, the Taliban, India, Osama bin Laden, and America. He has an impressive ability to jump from topic to topic. Easterners have a limitless capacity for gossip. I stay quiet.

"My friend, would you like some tea?"

"Thank you, sheikh."

"A sheikh wouldn't be in Wadi Kabir; he'd go to a big dealer."

I contemplate all the iron dead, piled up here so brutally. Car heads, eyes, feet, and iron intestines stare desperately at the cemetery around them and listen to death's last cry.

The Sad Donkey of Muscat

A blind man told me about the sad donkey of Muscat, which had narrated the city's stories to him.

I speak of Muscat, blind man, a city that lies between the mountains and the sea, between crushing poverty and obscene wealth, wealth as savage as a starving wolf, as painful as a woodcutter's ax. Packed with students, villagers, soldiers, informants, dreamers, merchants, Indians, beautiful and disappointed women, mosques, bars, embassies, dreams, disappointments, and contradictions. Muscat of exile and alienation, a stranger to itself. In Muscat you find everything and nothing. It's both mirage and meaning, the garden where children plant their dreams and also the forest that devours the children and their dreams. It's the ax that cuts and is cut off.

You see everything passing by silently in Muscat. Even the streets are silent. This city expands swiftly, but shrinks away from strangers, loss, and marginalization. The shadows of the dispossessed lengthen on its clean and cruel streets.

1

Through the sad donkey of Muscat, the dead narrator will tell tales of hunger, homelessness, and dispossession. From the harsh peaks of Bawshar, the donkey will see lands and sands devoured by highwaymen and the wolves of capitalism. From the mountains separating two neighborhoods, it will see city streets, bright lights stealing the lives of passersby, and cement forests eating away at history. Behind it will be another neighborhood asleep on the outskirts of Madinat al-Nahda, a hospital, a garden guarding its isolation, and eagles searching for prey to satisfy their eternal hunger.

2

The soldiers' rifles besiege you.
The tricks of light besiege you.
Follow the shadow of hunger,
And the sounds of childhood.
The grass dried up,
And the wind carried it far, far away.
Look for your lost voice in the mountains.
Look for your words scattered among the ancient
    trees.

3

Tonight the sad donkey of Muscat will go out with five friends with whom it spent its childhood exploring the streams, mountains, streets, and secluded corners of Madinat al-Nahda. The friends will celebrate New Year's Eve and the migration of their ancestors to the eastern mountains, perhaps stopping to nibble on snacks.

The donkey and its friends passed through a dry creek, reminiscing about their childhood. They saw cement boxes proliferating across the city. They cracked jokes about cars crossing asphalt valleys. They sang carols and the odes of their ancestors. They passed by schools, police cars, buses, and trees eaten up by drought. They saw an unmoving eagle at Al Hajar roundabout, sentenced by the municipality to direct passersby to the road of their dreams.

They crossed another roundabout and continued on to Wadi Adai bridge. At the last roundabout, they saw two horses pulling an iron cannon. The donkey said to its friends, "I don't know why the municipality didn't install two donkey statues on this roundabout. Donkeys have borne the hell of Al Amerat for years."

Coming down from a mountain peak, before the final turn, they saw a police checkpoint. They stood around for a while, swapping stories and waiting for the policemen to leave. Night fell, but the policemen stayed in place. The sad donkey of Muscat said, "What if we had a few drinks and got arrested for public intoxication? I bet there'd be front-page headlines the next morning, declaring, 'Six Drunk Donkeys Detained in Muscat Neighborhood.'"

From their vantage point, the friends could see an apartment balcony decorated with lights and red balloons. They watched an Indian family celebrating New Year's Eve, singing and drinking toasts. A young woman danced to her country's tunes.

The policemen didn't budge. The donkey and its friends returned disappointed to Madinat al-Nahda, cursing everything: Wadi Adai, New Year's Eve, the history of their ancestors.

4

After the inquisitive narrator had followed the life of Muscat's sad donkey for months, the donkey said to him, "I'll tell you the story of how my forefathers came to Muscat.

"In 1965, the Yemeni government requested a shipment of donkeys from Egypt. Yemen needed pack animals to transport weapons in rugged mountainous regions. The Egyptian government sent a ship full of donkeys to Yemen, but the winds blew it off course to the coast of Qurayyat, where it ran aground at dawn. Some sleeping fishermen woke up and helped the ship's crew, and a herd of donkeys came ashore as well. The herd fled to the springs of Qurayyat, some going even farther, all the way up to Al Amerat. As for what happened to the ship's crew, you'll have to ask the fishermen. Perhaps they can fill in the blanks of this incomplete story."

5

The blind man told us about the sad donkey of Muscat.

In the dark of the night, the donkey said about himself: "I was born on the margins and have lived on the city's outskirts, spending my life in distant shadows. On the margins I'll die. But before dying, blind man, I'll tell you about this country's marginalized people and the cement forests built by thieves and the oil springs drained by vipers in the desert. I'll tell you about the foreigner in Ruwi who renovates the Arabic language, and the martyrs and murderers who were killed twice by history, and the lies of light and the truth of shadows."

In the morning, the blind man regained his sight. He didn't see the donkey, but he saw his country shrouded in fear and hunger.

6

The blind man will tell you about the sad donkey that narrates forgotten stories about Muscat's lovers, lunatics, generals, and thieves; its beautiful and disgraced women; its lovelorn dreamers and the poets who walk its streets; its murderers, the English, and the Indians; its cemeteries and mosques; its invaders and the intellectuals who cozy up to power; a city bracketed between dream and illusion, and its new arrivals who dream only of accumulating more and more.

The blind man will fall asleep before the donkey finishes its story.

But the story will go on, with tedious details to which no one will pay any attention. It will come to a stop at a barricade between Al Amerat and Bawshar. You'll see monstrous forests of concrete, chasing away the sad donkey's last relatives. The donkey will pause at the edge of Al Tayeen mountains with tears in its eyes, looking at the hills of Al Amerat that expelled it from the homeland of its ancestors, who'd lived there for half a century. It will read aloud its last will and testament, and then leave the story and the place.

7

On the morning of January 9, before a single tear had fallen, before any laughter had bloomed, before the city had awakened, before any woman had said good morning to her husband, and before an inspiration had struck the governor, the sad donkey peered down from the mountains of Bawshar at slumbering Muscat clinging to its dreams and nightmares. It saw oil tankers leaving the port, a routine they have followed since the late 1960s. It saw a neighborhood with oil pipelines running through its belly. It saw the Gulf Hotel perched on Qurum Hilltop. At Qurum Beach it saw the feet of European women flirting with the morning sea.

The donkey turned its head slightly and saw the Ministry of Housing waving its flag and its nightmares. It gazed at the British embassy, which had guarded the Sea of Oman for two hundred years. The donkey didn't know if the kingdom whose sun never set was guarding the sea, or if the sea was guarding the embassy of ancient and modern pirates.

In the distance, it saw the Seeb market, with cars unloading their fish, dreams, and daily livelihoods. It took one last look around, thinking to itself: this is your Muscat, with its fluttering flags and dreams.

The sad donkey turned around with tears in its eyes. It saw Al Amerat beginning to stir with the languor of a rose that blooms unhurriedly in the morning. It saw Al Amerat as it was during the 1940s, a small village. It saw the caravans of merchants, travelers, and frightened people standing still. It looked again at Al Amerat and saw immigrants streaming in from Nizwa and the mountain villages, carrying their dreams and digging a flowing *falaj*. The teary-eyed donkey saw shepherds crossing silent paths and contemplating the isolation of the place. It looked at the rooftop dishes that collected sounds and images. It passed by children waiting for a school bus and workers cracking jokes over their morning tea at a café. It saw a nurse in white clothes start the engine of her car and her dreams. Without crying or screaming, it began to run toward Madinat al-Nahda. Then, it climbed the Al Tayeen mountains, bidding farewell to everything.

The White Goat's Head

At six in the morning, I try to lift my head weighed down by nightmares. In a dream, I'd seen military boots trample on the head of a martyr whose picture I'd seen on social media a day ago, killed on the street, standing tall like an Arabian palm tree. Her eyes were as clear as a mountain spring. She was alone when a soldier's bullet defiled her. In my dream, I also saw Nakata, Murakami's hero in *Kafka on the Shore*, the homeless old man living on welfare in Tokyo's Nakano district, who speaks to city cats haunted by hunger, poverty, and oblivion.

In the next room, a sleeping child holds a plastic gun in his hand, its muzzle below the bed. I look at my immigrant neighbor's garden, its dry trees, and the sleeping child holding his gun waiting for birds to land on the neighbor's trees. Neither has the neighbor returned from her African homeland, nor have the birds landed on the dry tree branches, nor has the child woken up to target the birds with his plastic gun.

s

Driving on a Bawshar mountain road, on the way to slumbering Muscat, I remember Saeed bin Khalfan al-Khalili at the moment he stepped into history,[1] coming down from the mountains with his army to wash away the dust of oblivion from the throne. History is a complex game. I look for the right music and find that André Rieu suits my descent down Bawsher's mountains and sands. Rieu makes an entrance with his heavenly music as I drive down the slopes of my text. Saeed bin Khalfan al-Khalili descends the slopes with his soldiers, while I descend the mountains with Rieu. It's the same historical moment, with music and an army of the country's homeless surrounding Muscat.

s

Seven in the morning:

In my dreams, I always manage to lose my white shoes. I take them off now to walk on the beach. Clouds are blowing in from the Indian Ocean, resembling the eighteenth-century ships of the church's predatory pirates, coveting the prize and magic of the East. I hear the pirates singing hymns and war songs. I walk a bit more. Some tourists are dragging their feet over the sand. A European woman raises her phone to photograph some unusual cloud formations. A police car goes by. Are the policemen guarding the beach from the pirate ships?

Under the Love Street bridge, people have documented their sorrows and longings for their beloveds in different languages: Arabic, English, Balochi, Hindi. Some have written their lovers' names on the pillar that carries Love Street on its back. Do the absent objects of their desire also carry a bridge, a street, and love?

I hurry back to my white shoes so the pirates won't steal them like the woman in my dream. The pirate ships approach Muscat's shore. On my way back, I see the head of a white goat in the sand. Who ate the goat's body by the sea, but left the head behind? The slaughtered goat's eyes look fearfully at the sea and the approaching pirate ships. The abandoned head won't drink seawater. Two tears fall from the goat's eyes and disappear in the sand.

Morning beachgoers begin to drown out the sounds of the sleeping city's sea.

s

Eight in the morning:

At the beach café, I put Kafka on the table. Elderly European ladies are bathing the sea with their noise and shadows. Children undress and play, reconstructing their dreams in sand.

"Aren't they cold?" a young man sitting behind me asks.

"These people are accustomed to the snows of Europe. Muscat's January chill is nothing for them," I reply.

He starts talking about how cold it is up on Jabal Akhdar. Then, he introduces himself as an Omani of Palestinian origin.

"My family was displaced from Haifa to Beirut. Our house is still in Haifa; my grandfather still has the key. We came to Oman in the late sixties. My father worked as a teacher in Samail."

I don't know why this man is telling his story to a stranger in a café. I remain silent so the trees of his tales don't bloom and I don't fall into strangers' traps. I look at the elderly Buckingham ladies (as the late novelist Ali al-Maamari used to call them),[2] each holding her coffee cup and dragging out her years of boredom, loneliness, and joy. I remember the Omani mothers and grandmothers of my childhood getting together like this, carrying their dates, coffee, and stories. The elderly Buckingham ladies have no dates, only the dry biscuits of their distant land.

The beach begins to fill up with people and stories: a woman chasing children's laughter with her phone camera, a sixtysomething man reading aloud the biography of his childhood to the sea, a teenager pampering her white English bulldog with a morning treat, taxi drivers seeking their livelihood from tourists. The stranger's eyes stalk the pirates approaching from the Indian Ocean.

I pick up Kafka and his cats and drive back home to work some more on Muscat's sad donkey. Birds have ravaged the neighbor's garden while my little pirate slept, dreaming that his plastic pistol had been stolen.

s

What the Dead Goat Said . . .

Greetings, passersby through this transient text. I want to clarify what the narrator wrote about me. I can confirm that this man walked by me on the morning of January 25, more precisely at 7:30 a.m. He noticed my head abandoned on the beach, looked at me for a few minutes, and then moved on toward the bridge. There, he examined the pillars and read some graffiti. After that he went to a café and read a few pages of his book. Then, as he's written above, he left to go home and write about Muscat's sad donkey.

I know I'm dead, but let me tell you what I witnessed that night.

The ships that the narrator saw and compared to marauding schooners actually belong to modern pirates, not from the eighteenth century, but contemporary ones, thieves of modernity, money, and oil, with advanced tools to plunder things, cultures, and livelihoods. They unloaded their dreams on the beach, slaughtered me, and walked away.

They sang for a little while on the beach and danced to the songs of modernity. With tears, they recalled the Portuguese, English, and French ships that sailed past this shore. Then, they took their wine and food and moved on, leaving my head here, alone, guarding the Muscat night.

Pirates of Wadi Adai

He finally got out of bed after hours of staring at the ceiling in a fierce battle with insomnia. Sleep eluded him, even though he wasn't sick or in prison, neither in debt nor a creditor, neither in love nor beloved, neither betrayer nor betrayed. After puttering around for a bit, he went downstairs to his basement office. He switched on the light and flipped open his laptop. On the blank page, he typed: *Why are they laughing?*

> In this city—which welcomes you with a cemetery of its dead, including the immigrants who died without money for a funeral, or a coffin in which to fly back to their countries; and bids you farewell with an insane asylum—how can people laugh, trapped as they are between the dead and the insane? Not just that, but how do they even find time for laughter?

A weak beginning for a text written at night about boredom, he said to himself. He tried to rephrase the paragraph, to prune the narrative and cut out superfluous verbs to match its sluggish feel. Before deleting each word, he asked himself: Does boredom stem from the city's mood

38

or from existence itself? Can a city be bored, or do cities feel nothing at all? Aren't these mere illusions that writers and poets project onto inanimate objects to humanize them and escape the censor's scissors or society's jibes?

Above all, can language reshape the mood of bored cities?

s

He deleted the first three words, *in this city*, thinking: the reader knows very well that every city has its dead, madmen, foreigners, and immigrants. The repetitiveness of the text bothered him. He reviewed the two questions, and then tried to add a third despite knowing that the people of his city hated questions, were terrified of them. They'd been looking for answers since they'd been in their mothers' wombs, digging up ready-made responses to questions of death and the grave. At school, the teachers would warn students against asking questions, saying, "Whoever asks about something that doesn't concern him will find something that doesn't satisfy him." Of course, being beaten or thrown out of class never satisfied anyone. At the mosque, the imam would recite Quranic verses that cautioned against questions. In this city, people would even try to memorize the answers to questions for job interviews. Why then do I burden this minor and ephemeral text with questions that the city doesn't like, this city that fights questions and considers them a threat to itself and its people, history, and sacred symbols? Let the question soar above the skies of cities that love and care for it, not those that slaughter it in its cradle.

There's no harm in asking another question so that the dead city will awaken.

—Who guards the city?

—They do.

—Who are they?

—There, in the fort, up on the mountain.

s

He scratched the tip of his nose (which didn't resemble Gogol's) and thought of a different, smoother, beginning to the weariness of a besieged city. He remembered that he'd had another idea in his head when he turned on the laptop. As he was coming downstairs to his basement (which certainly didn't resemble Dostoyevsky's), he'd wanted to write about the feelings of a woman in a cancer hospital waiting for chemotherapy. From her bed, the woman saw a child at the end of a long corridor. The corridor had no windows or doors, as if the doctors were locking pain away until it curdled in their patients' souls, or as if they were shutting out the laughter from a nearby playground so it wouldn't sneak into children's hearts. From her white bed in the white corridor, the woman stared at the child, listening to her laughter. It was about this fleeting moment, heavy with pain and emotion, that he wanted to write. And it was in this white corridor resembling life that he wanted to narrate stories for the woman awaiting death. Not about the pain she felt. Pain is difficult, if not impossible, to put in writing. Rather, he was thinking of capturing the moment when the woman looked at the child at the end of the corridor, the moment laughter crept into her soul exhausted by illness, doctors' appointments, white corridors, frowning faces, the night sounds of medical equipment, and the red light above her bed. He didn't have the cinematic tools to capture the moment, but he felt it, as if he himself were the one looking at the little girl.

During the five minutes that the woman was waiting for her turn in the chemo room, she recalled the story of her life. Does pain remind us of life, or of death, and is it necessary to connect pain with death? Are five minutes enough to recollect all of life's details, to reach all the feelings embedded within human memory? She remembered her four children at home, her husband with a heart ravaged by sorrow, her faraway childhood, and school friends who'd become emotionally distant as they dispersed across the country. She remembered the trees in her yard that she'd cared for and developed a spiritual relationship with twenty years ago.

When the little girl laughed, the woman with leukemia said, "Where did I forget my laughter, dear life?"

Life was uncaring; it ignored the question of the woman in a long corridor awaiting dawn and death.

The woman picked up her phone and typed a note:

Dear night, what are you doing to a dying woman in a cancer ward's corridors?

What are you doing to the soul of a man who won't find his wife in the morning?

How will you wipe away the child's tears when he returns in the evening and doesn't find anyone to open the door to home and life?

Who will dry the tears of the trees at night?

As she wrote, she looked at the remains of the henna rose on the palm of her hand. She remembered the roses in her garden, on her bedroom curtains, and on the anniversary of their first night together. Tonight she was contemplating the painting on the corridor wall, even though she'd seen it more than once. She looked at the pond in the painting, surrounded by palm trees and rocks. For the first time, she saw children swimming in the pond. To distract herself from the waiting and pain, she listened to the children's laughter. There were four of them. She sang to them, but at first they were too engrossed in their game to pay attention to her voice. Then they began to listen to the singing of the woman waiting in a long corridor, and the more they listened to her singing, the more they cried. A few white birds perched on the branches of the palm trees by the pond, while others flew over the mountains, in the picture hanging on the corridor wall of the cancer ward.

s

He wanted to write about this moment, this look of a cancer-stricken woman at a little girl laughing at the end of a white corridor. The woman wrote at the right time— at night—and in the right place: an empty corridor that plunged into whiteness, even as the pain plunged into her soul.

He didn't know how his idea turned into a text about a city besieged by the dead, madmen, and foreigners or how the idea of the text itself changed.

None of this is important. All beautiful and painful things change.

He slept for a while, thinking about another beginning for "Why are they laughing?" He dreamed of the dead streaming out of the cemetery, pleading with the living to stop crowding them. He saw them marching in a huge procession. Some took advantage of the opportunity to visit their homes and greet their families, while others went to the city's *falaj* to rinse off the cemetery dust and their memories. Yet others went for a walk in the park, leaving behind roses for friends who'd forgotten them. Only the children refused to leave their cemetery, preferring instead to play the games death had stolen from them. Some began to chant songs they'd learned when they were alive, while others traced their mothers' faces in the dirt. A girl in school clothes stood at the cemetery entrance. She peeked into the custodian's room, moved aside the window curtain, and started singing to the guardian of the city of the dead. He laughed in his sleep. She picked up a black pebble and scrawled on the wall: "The sleeper guards the dead, and the dead cling to the sleeping guard's dream." Then she returned to the cemetery.

Some of the dead started a petition against the pirates of Wadi Adai who desecrate the city's tranquility by crossing the wadi, bathing in the pools, and holding loud parties at night. The dead delivered the signed petition to the police station. The police were terrified when they saw the dead approach.

Meanwhile, the madmen escaped from the asylum, despite the locked doors, guards, and cameras. They organized themselves in straight files and marched through the streets. People paid no attention to their chants. A few stray dogs accompanied the insane marchers to amuse themselves after they'd tired of chasing the sounds of night and hunger. They kept the madmen in line and suppressed the unruly with their barking. Banners were raised asking for the asylum director to be fired. Some of the lunatics got carried away and started to demand the governor's dismissal, while others went further still and insisted that the police chief be ousted. The dogs were terrified when they heard the police chief's name and tried to appease the madmen's anger. When the protest march approached the stone-eagle roundabout by the police station, some of the strays ran off, while others tried to hide among the crowd.

He was immersed in the dream, watching what the madmen and the dead would do to the city, and what the pirates of Wadi Adai would do when they saw this terrifying night.

s

Crying loudly, the woman opened the door, giving him a scare. What made her cry, especially at this late hour? He tried to determine if he was dreaming in bed or working in his basement office. He asked the woman, "What's making you cry in the middle of the night? Did someone die?"

She couldn't stop weeping. He tried to speak but couldn't.

The woman shook him by the shoulder. He asked himself who was dead and who was insane on this night of madness. But she wasn't like the woman waiting for her chemotherapy session. Sobbing, she said to him, "Why did you die?"

"I didn't die! I'm right here in front of you," he said. He closed the laptop so the dead and the insane wouldn't overhear his conversation with the crying woman and she wouldn't see his nighttime funeral.

"But I saw you! You died in a traffic accident, and your funeral was at night," she said, after convincing herself that he was real.

He heard the voices of the dead from the screen, protesting that the cemetery couldn't accommodate anyone else, and they wouldn't tolerate any more disturbing night funerals. Had the woman heard the sounds from the screen, or was she really just making sure he wasn't dead?

"What are these nightmares of yours?" he said gently. "This is me before you, neither sick nor in prison. Just suffering from insomnia."

He went to the kitchen to get her a glass of cold water. Before he returned to the woman who'd seen him dead in her nightmare, distant voices floated in from the kitchen window. "Oh my God, they're getting closer," he said to himself. "I don't know if it's the insane, the dead, or the pirates of Wadi Adai." Quickly, he shut the window.

The woman turned to leave after making sure that she'd only had a nightmare and the man was alive and well in his basement office. But she was uncertain if he was dreaming or waiting fearfully for what the creatures would do to the city.

Before leaving, she said, "Don't forget to shut the hallway door."

He stretched his legs across the table, flipped the laptop open, and looked again at "Why are they laughing?"

S

The woman about to enter the chemo room said good-bye to the four children, who dove into the pond in the painting on the silent corridor wall. The white birds flew away, leaving behind an empty landscape.

S

He remained hesitant, contemplative, in pain, afraid of the weary city, suffocated by nightmares of night and life.

He slept a little. The dream and the city's scenery changed. The madmen handed the governor a strongly worded protest, demanding that the asylum be relocated from this boring city to one blooming with life. They asked for the right to enjoy their lives in private and to hold elections at the asylum. They complained about certain inhumane practices against them and demanded that the asylum director be fired.

The dead gathered at the cemetery's outskirts. The custodian didn't pay attention to what was happening around him. After his nap, he was busy watching a movie on television. The dead gathered for reasons unknown to the dreamer watching the crowds from the basement of his house on the city's outskirts and to the custodian watching a movie while sending flirtatious WhatsApp messages.

Meanwhile, the madmen went off to the *falaj* to quench their thirst for life. The pirates lurking in Wadi

Adai readied their ships crowded with invaders, generals, Englishmen, Persians, Portuguese, Indians, and the turbaned ones. For years they'd been anticipating such events, setting traps for the lies of history. Under Wadi Adai's bridges they rewrote their past. Water flowed under the bridges, but they didn't worry, well aware that more water would flow, satiating their thirst and bringing them new dreams. They knew that every era has its invaders and pirates, and that the bridges that carry pedestrians also have at their roots history, traps, and the memory of water.

What brought all these people together in one place, on one night? How did Wadi Adai expand to accommodate these bizarre contradictions? Would these ships carry the country's madmen and its dead?

That's not for us to know. Reality can be stranger than dreams or fiction. Events sometimes happen without order or regularity, which spoil the wonder of things.

People paid no attention to the crowds gathering on the city's outskirts on their way to climb the mountains overlooking Muscat. The dreamer didn't ask what kept the people of the city so busy. Did they consciously ignore the crowds and not have the courage to ask who they were? Or were they afraid of questions?

The crowds passed by a woman's funeral but didn't stop or pay attention to the night of mourning. The custodian opened the cemetery gate. Everyone heard the crying of four children, their father, and several relatives. The crying didn't stop the crowds from climbing the mountains without participating in burial rituals.

The pirates and their ambitions ascended swiftly. The madmen were tired not just of the road but also of life and its pain. The dead dreamed only of looking down over the sea. At the summit, they saw an imposing fort defending Muscat. There, they stopped to gaze at the lights, the streets, the sea, and the people leaving their homes and dreams. Just before dawn, they returned to their graves, saying, "Muscat can't even bear the living, so how can it tolerate us?"

The pirates, however, didn't stop. They climbed up to the fort, besieged it, broke into its rooms, wrote their slogans on the walls, and marveled at the country's history and dreams that had been locked away. As for the madmen, they continued on to the park. They'd come to hate high walls, fleeing from the barriers of life to the walls of the asylum. Some ordered coffee at a shrine by the sea. The fort was completely under the pirates' control as dawn approached, while the madmen thronged Muscat's streets. Some slept under bridges; others settled down by Ministries Street, using as pillows banners emblazoned with their demands.

Disagreements broke out among the pirates. The Portuguese and the Persians wanted to divide the sea, the port, and history among themselves. The Indians went to Mutrah and Ruwi to take over the markets and practice their trade. The turbaned ones liked the seat of power and the fort overlooking the city. But they became impatient and retreated from the mountaintop, getting lost on the way down. The English alone continued to latch on to the country's jugular and drink its blood. "We're here!" they proclaimed. People ran away in fear. In the end, only the English remained at the fort, directing affairs from high above.

Next morning, the newspapers declared an official holiday. The streets were blocked and schools and ministries were closed because of the madmen thronging Muscat. They gathered on bridges to hang up their demands. The police chased them around, rounding them up in buses whose blue bore no resemblance to the sea. Some sneaked into the small room under Wadi Adai bridge after putting up banners demanding that the governor grant them the right to live.

At four in the morning, the man who'd been dreaming of writing about the city's night turned off his laptop. He saw hanging on a city bridge the title of his text: "Why are they laughing?" Under it he saw a woman's funeral, pirate ships, the dead, the insane, and a cemetery custodian.

He followed his wife's instructions and shut the hallway door. In the bedroom he found the dead woman and her four children.

The Storybird Eats
the Fish of Mutrah

Birds Fleeing the Imagination

That afternoon, I was on the way to Al Amerat industrial area, driving on what seemed to be the road to hell. On my right I saw a junkyard, where the municipality had abandoned lampposts too decrepit to illuminate blind alleys, and also road signs for villages consumed by oblivion, forsaken by people, and displaced by drought. I saw barrels of waste left to rot on this earthly inferno. Mountains guarded the junkyard, and were themselves guarded by the solitude of long-vanished shepherds.

In the middle of the junkyard stood a neglected globe. On the globe's scorching surface, rivers, oceans, and springs dried up; forests, fields, and hearts withered; music and dreams went silent; lovers' desires turned to ash; tyrants fell from their thrones; and other tyrants arose amid blood and devastation. All that has happened and is happening on this earth did not disturb the globe abandoned in the municipal junkyard.

I saw a flock of birds land on the globe, which the municipality had removed from a renovated roundabout and discarded at the junkyard. Upon my approach, the birds crept into a withered forest. I stopped the car and got out to look for them. I put my hand on the coast of Spain, but failed to catch the birds. Instead, I saw mirages. I saw forests ablaze and books of history, poetry, and illusion in flames. I saw palaces, singers, and caliphs who'd abandoned their dreams. I heard Lorca reciting his last poems against the dictator. I saw the dictator caressing a bullet to put in the heart of the broken revolutionary poet.

The moment I put my hands on the tree behind which the flock of birds had vanished, I heard a caravan of camels crossing the Empty Quarter, led by Mubarak bin London on a quest for life's joys.[1] Riding with him were two young men from southern Oman. Accompanying them was the sound of the desert, its eternal silence, and white men's dreams, drawn up at the intelligence agencies. I held onto the tree trunk so the birds wouldn't escape. When I shook the trunk, Bin London's story didn't fall out. I don't know where the English gentleman hid half of the story.

I turned slightly to the east to follow what Bin London was doing in the Arabian desert. I saw him sitting under a *ghāf* tree while the two young men made coffee. The English gentleman began to tell them about his very clean and civilized country, his childhood, his mother's grave in the English countryside, and the beauty of Englishwomen. A cloud of smoke from his pipe mingled with the smell of coffee. The smoke from his mouth disturbed the flock of birds resting in the tree providing shade to the white man's dreams in the Empty Quarter.

While the Englishman was telling his young fellow travelers stories about his dog-loving country, the birds flew away. I was too busy listening to Mubarak bin London to notice where they went.

After looking around for a while, I found the birds perched on the branches of a lonesome tree under which sat a man ravaged by questions and the anxiety of knowledge. The birds didn't know what the man was thinking, or why he was sitting by himself. Failing to get his attention by chirping, they dropped some fruit on him. An apple fell on the worried man's head.

The man screamed and raved, and then he picked up the apple and flung it at the birds. The apple that had fallen from the lonesome tree on the head of the man sitting by himself didn't resemble Eve's apple, or the apple of love, or the apple of iPhones sliced by the knife of capitalism, nor did it resemble the anxiety of the man who'd been sitting by himself.

After the birds had flown off to other skies and forests, people didn't wonder who'd dropped the apple, but rather began repeating the man's words. The birds no longer thought about questions, and I stopped looking for them when they flew off with the story to a nearby mountain, ignoring the scream of a worker guarding the municipal junkyard.

Two Fish of Mutrah

Nobody paid attention to the statues of two fish in the middle of a roundabout in Mutrah. The fish didn't tempt a fisherman to take them home so his children could play with them, or so his wife could cook a delicious meal for the family. Housewives from distant villages going to Mutrah's souk didn't sympathize with the fish either, and the cameras of female European tourists seduced by the market ignored them as well.

Only a hungry black cat standing on the sidewalk thought about crossing the street to stand atop one of the fish and narrate the story of its Indian lineage, about how it became a homeless vagabond in Mutrah when its family in Ruwi abandoned it to return to New Delhi so the daughter could study filmmaking, which she'd dreamed of doing ever since she was a student at the Indian school in Darsait.

The cat stood on the sidewalk, annoying the two fish with its slightly embellished autobiography. Pedestrians, tourists, ships, and fish at the port of Mutrah paid no attention to the cat's stories.

The two fish questioned the cat about its country's seas, fish, and whales. The cat began to sing and weep nostalgically.

The fish closest to the sea told the cat about its eternal longing for water. "At night, when Mutrah and its souk, pirates, and ships are asleep, I get bored and sing to the sea. Perhaps the sea will pay attention to my voice. One night, I was singing and crying when a fisherman passed by. He screamed and ran away."

As the fish was talking, a bird flew down from one of the enormous ships docked in the port and landed on its head. The bird, which had just finished a sumptuous supper, blithely relieved itself on the fish's head, with no regard for the serious conversation among the two fish and their guest, the black cat.

The fish on the side of Saidia School said angrily to its companions, "What do you expect from a bird that eats scraps off ships and fishermen, a bird that abandoned its voice and ran off to beg from strangers?"

The bird flew off to take a nap on the roof of the fish market and wait for fishermen to come in with their catch.

The black cat said to itself, "What should I do with a bored, lonely, neglected fish with a soiled head?" Looking neither right nor left, it approached the roundabout, intending to climb the surrounding fence.

Without any fuss, the speeding wheels of a passing police car ran over the black cat as it was on its way to clean the fish's head soiled by the bird from the enormous ship.

The eyes of a dead cat by the roundabout in Mutrah saw two policemen placing parking tickets on windshields. They also saw two men sitting by the Great Prophet Mosque discussing a looming war. Just before the black cat's soul departed, it thought about the girl now studying filmmaking at an Indian university.

When the two policemen were done with their task of ticketing illegally parked cars, they passed again by the roundabout—now with two weeping fish—paying no attention to the black cat's decapitated head. The two fish heard the driver of the police car say to his partner, "I have a long way to go to Al Batinah."

His partner replied, "I have a long way to go to Al Sharqiya."

The fish with the soiled head said to itself, "What do the long ways to Al Batinah and Al Sharqiya have to do with a black cat getting run over by a police car?" Then it went silent.

A European woman looking out from the third-floor balcony of the Breeze Hotel had seen the cat get run over, as if she were watching a documentary on feline history.

s

That night, the people of Mutrah heard two fish singing to a dead cat.

The French Ship's Dog

The French flag had been flying on the cruise ship docked in Mutrah's port for five days—so the waiter at the café by the souk entrance told me. The ship's passengers disembarked each morning, unraveling their laughter, their phone cameras, their amazement at the fine details of the sites, penetrating Muscat's body, its museums and mosques, into the dark of the souk and the whiteness of the buildings, into the questions posed by forts and towers. At night they returned to the ship to lie in their beds and flick through the photos piled up on their phones, laughing at their own cold smiles frozen on the screens. On the ship was a bored black dog, left all day with the ship's security guard while its owner went off to explore the city.

For the first three days, the dog would crane its neck, staring at the buildings standing firm and tall, as if they were guarding the corniche. It saw people walking along the seafront: tourists, policemen, taxi drivers, café-goers, disappointed lovers. The smell of fresh fish wafted into its nose. It heard the call to prayer and gazed at the mosque's blue minaret, tempted by the bustle of people entering and leaving the souk, wishing it could swim ashore and use a snack on the corniche as an excuse to avoid a scolding from its owner.

The dog barked several times, trying to attract the attention of passersby along the shore. But nobody paid any attention to the barking of a lonely dog standing on the deck of a ship under a French flag flapping in the sea breeze. Disappointed with this country's people, the dog stretched out its paws under the guard's chair, head buried between legs. The guard was immersed in a song playing on his phone. To cheer up his canine companion, he went to the galley, took a piece of meat from the refrigerator, and put it on a plate to give to the dog.

After eating what was on offer, the dog lifted its paws up to the railing and stared once again at the buildings, trying to spell out the foreign words: Saidia School, Breeze Hotel, Lawatia Walled Quarter, Great Prophet Mosque, Anna Café, Mutrah Souk.

The dog's imagination began to weave a dialogue between the scene's various characters. What if a Saidia School student tried to tease a European tourist drinking her morning coffee in her pajamas on the balcony of a room at the Breeze Hotel? "Hiiiii, I love you!" he shouted, in English, from the window of his classroom.

The phrase reached the tourist's ears as she was enjoying her Mutrah morning. She smiled, looked out at the sea, and saw a man sitting in front of the Great Prophet Mosque. Clasping her coffee and her morning moment, she uttered a sentence in broken Arabic, "May the peace, blessings, and mercy of God be upon you."

The man sitting in front of the Great Prophet Mosque looked around for the person who had spoken but saw no one. He walked toward the souk entrance, ordered himself a cup of tea, and began to stare at the seagulls.

Neither the student, nor the tourist, nor the man sitting in front of the mosque noticed the barking dog on the French cruise ship.

At noon, the guard served lunch to the bored dog, and then sat down again, legs stretched lazily, losing himself once again to music. The dog watched the flocks of seagulls intoxicated by tourists' cameras and the breadcrumbs thrown their way by some of Mutrah's lovers.

On the afternoon of the fourth day, while the guard was in the galley drowsily listening to his songs, the dog decided to slip away and explore the sites. It jumped over the railing into the water and almost drowned before managing to paddle over to the buildings by the fish market. In a square behind the market that the municipality had forgotten to develop, the dog from the French cruise ship began to run around, head raised, chasing clouds. It stretched out on a cement patch that the port workers used to play cricket.

A murder of crows on the fish market's roof watched the foreign dog's joy and became unsettled. They cawed clamorously, and every single crow in Mutrah answered their call. The crows flew low over the forgotten square behind the fish market to tease the dog. The dog barked. The crows intensified their antics, flying over the dog's

back and cawing loudly. The dog ran off, barking in surprise at the crows' attack despite their shared blackness. It
tried to seek refuge under a lonesome tree at the edge of
the square. But the crows did not relent, landing on the
tree, crowding its branches. The dog thought, "How will I
get back to the ship and escape this country's crows? Oh
my God, why are these crows frightened of a bored, lonely
dog's fleeting joy?"

The dog decided to confront its tormentors. It started
running around the square, dancing with its front paws
raised, balancing on its hind legs, ignoring the raucous
racket that the black birds were making.

The crows were amazed by the dog's dancing. They
flew off in surprise to perch again on the fish market's
roof. Never in their history had they seen a dog from this
country dancing! Grudging buds of friendship began to
sprout between them and the dog. They descended from
their amazement and the fish market's roof. The dog
stopped dancing and began to examine its surroundings:
forts atop mountains, huge ships resembling mountains
in the harbor. It tried to ask the crows about the ships, but
the crows were afraid of the dog's loaded question.

On the square's western edge was a tree under which
five men in identical clothing sat with their backs against
a crumbling wall, staring at the sea, the void, and the giant
ships, swearing loudly. In front of them were bottles of
water and soft drinks. The dog was surprised by the men's
glares, amazed by the smoke coming out of their mouths.

The crows asked the dog about its country.

"My country is far away, across the seas. There are crows and clean streets there, and I have a home and a family," the dog replied.

The crows marveled at the dog's French life. The only dogs they knew were Mutrah's strays, which slept in underpasses and mountain passes, and struggled to sate their nightly hunger from garbage bins. Impressed by the dog, the crows asked more questions about its life and what it was doing in Mutrah.

The dog told them it was guarding the cruise ship and accompanying its owner, a Frenchwoman traveling around the world. It blithely mentioned owning a passport. The crows were even more astonished. A dog with a passport, a home, a family! The crows knew that the people of this country didn't have passports—in fact, some had never even left the capital, while others had never entered it.

When the dog asked the crows about food, they were confused by the question. One replied that they ate from the garbage, or stole fish from the nearby market.

The dog enjoyed talking with Mutrah's crows. For the first time ever, someone had asked about its life. Eventually, the crows flew off in search of dinner. The dog continued its frolicking in the forgotten square behind the fish market. It looked around and saw cranes that lifted nothing but emptiness after work at the port had come to a halt. At the foot of the mountain, on the western side, it saw a police station and a fluttering flag with daggers and swords. The police station guarded the sea from pirates. Numerous cats were dispersed across the corniche, lazing at the edges of the fish market, on the streets, in front of the Asian restaurants. The dog tried to arrange the scattered images in its mind: mosque, market, school, hotels, sea, forts, crows, cats, police station, workers, dogs, tourists, taxi drivers, silent port. What was this absurdity? How could all these contradictions coexist in one picture?

The dog tried to recall its French life: how it used to wake up languidly in the morning, the strictly scheduled meals, monthly visits to the vet for checkups, walks on Parisian streets with its owner. Everything in that life was orderly—even dogs were entitled to streets, parks, clinics, cemeteries, bank accounts.

None of that mattered. Perhaps the comparisons were unfair. "They have their lives, and we have ours," the dog thought to itself.

Before sunset it returned to the ship. The guard still hadn't emerged from his sleep and songs. The dog's mind was full of thoughts, images, contradictions.

At night, after fatigue and sleep had fully penetrated the bodies of the ship's crew and passengers, the dog walked over to the edge of deck. It watched Mutrah's lights reflected in the water, and began to fantasize, thinking about what the crows had said, imagining a life other than one of slavery.

"It's true that I have a privileged life," the dog thought. "But I remain the Frenchwoman's guard and servant. What if I were to decide to escape this life of laws and slavery? But how would I live here? I have no friends, no food, no home. What about my friends back in Paris? How would I contact them? Is there a post office here?"

The thought of rebellion and escape began to unnerve the dog. It remembered its childhood, how it had been pampered, enrolled in dog school to learn the ways of guarding and dealing with the wealthy, how to be obedient to its human masters. Midnight fell upon Mutrah, but anxiety had robbed all traces of sleep from the French dog's eyes.

Nostalgia for the life it used to live assailed the dog, together with unease about the life it now intended to lead. The ship's passengers dove into the placid lakes of their dreams, while the dog tossed and turned in the volcanoes of memory and anxiety. A sound came from the blue minaret. The dog liked the sound, and it liked the ambience of approaching dawn. It saw people entering the mosque.

The next morning, the dog did not leave the ship, dozing on and off throughout the day.

Darkness fell once again. The dog resolved to escape by dawn.

Before the morning call to prayer had rung out over Mutrah, the dog was in the square where it had played with the crows. It passed by the tree under which it had seen the five men. It saw four of them asleep, while the fifth babbled incoherently. The dog ran past the fish market, where it saw fresh catch being brought in. Near the Fish roundabout, as a cool morning breeze picked up, it felt the need to hurry before someone on the ship noticed its absence. It ran past Saidia School, the mosque, the souk entrance; it ran along the deserted corniche. Rounding a curve, it crossed the street, climbed up to the fort, and sneaked inside, exhausted. At six in the morning, it saw the ship with the fluttering French flag leaving the port.

The Guardian of Muscat

"Why are you awake at this hour, guardian?"

"To guard Muscat, of course."

"Muscat is no longer what it was long ago, a city of hunger, thirst, and wars. But where can it go anyway? Your Muscat is trapped between mountains and the sea. It both wounds and is wounded, a fugitive from itself."

"But I was once the city's guardian, with the key to its heart in my hand. I was the one who ushered in the dawn after its disturbing nightmares and closed out the day's fatigue and weariness. Who are you to abolish my job, my life, my dreams?"

"I hope you return to your eternal sleep. Muscat's heart is no longer what you used to hold in your hand. It has expanded to make room for all, turning colorless, odorless, leaning toward the sea in its fragility, accepting foreigners, murderers, lovers, municipal workers, students, nurses, policemen, and cemeteries. Yet, at the same time, it has shrunk, becoming cramped for poems, dreams, labor unions, and writings by dreamers about people and migrants."

"Stop, please, no more. I'm very thirsty."

"Alas, the *falaj* dried up a long time ago, consumed by modernity and police stations."

s

From his tiny room that time had forgotten, the guardian—who'd been dead for more than forty years—imagined that he still kept Muscat's gate, the only outlet for the dreams of the tribes and the poor, those oppressed between two competing powers, or fleeing famine. Time didn't allow the dead guardian to feel the ecstasy of power, the power of doors open and closed, of the fear he'd once exercised over those who passed through his gate.

His entire life was tied to that gate, so much so that he'd earned the nickname Friend of the Gate in his youth. But the gate was always closed in his dreams, and its key didn't give him the ability to travel far. He'd wishfully imagined that the key was his, but it belonged to others, for he himself was never permitted to leave.

That afternoon, he left his forgotten room under Wadi Adai bridge and sat in the shade of a *sidra* tree. He started talking to passersby. "Who raised this wall? Why didn't you wake me up? Where have you been all this time? Remember the wall at Wadi Adai crossing that stopped people from entering Muscat, the wall that stood between the lives of people from inner Oman and those in exile, separating dreams from hunger?"

He looked up to gaze at the *sidra*. It made him happy, this last remnant of what he'd once guarded. He felt like hugging the tree. He wished he could make a stick out of one of its branches to drive away the nightmares and noise that besieged him.

"Where have the caravans from inner Oman gone?" he asked himself. "Camels, donkeys, and people used to shelter under this tree. I would listen to their stories, learn about cities, villages, and roads that I'd never heard of; about a war on the mountain and airplanes from far away; about the wounded, martyrs, enemies, traitors, and tribes; and about oil companies exploring the desert. I could see sweat running down their faces. I don't know why I didn't feel the pain of all those people. What blinded me and froze my heart, just like this city and the lives and dreams of its people?

"I listened to their dreams, not understanding what working abroad meant to them, or why they insisted on leaving their villages. They were young, dreaming of a piece of paper that Muscat would grant so they could leave. True, I wasn't rich. I never imagined I would live away from Muscat. I didn't feel their hunger or poverty. Oh, where did I abandon my heart?"

s

From the shade of the lonely *sidra*, the guardian contemplated his surroundings, listening to the voices of passersby. He understood some but not all the dialects and languages, never having heard some of them before. He looked at passing birds, flying in different directions, some toward the Wadi Hattat building, others toward the mountains behind Nahda Hospital. He saw cars driving toward Wadi Adai. Under the bridge he saw relaxing workers playing with their phones. He didn't understand what was happening. He was thirsty, but decided to wait a little and take another nap. Perhaps one of the caravans of memory would pass by. He listened to the stories of taxi drivers, which were unlike any stories he'd heard when he'd been a guardian, guarding everything except stories. He heard their anger about rising gas prices, taxes, parking tickets, the bills that appeared every month, the companies that competed with them for their daily living, the tall tales of passersby and foreigners who claimed to know Muscat better than they did.

"You haven't changed, Muscat. Hunger has been besieging you since my time, the time of the gate," the guardian whispered to himself after overhearing the stories.

The British company Shell had put up a sign for a gas station across from his small room. He glared at the yellow sign: "500 meters," he read. A blackbird landed on the Shell sign. It stared at the guardian and the story. The guardian saw a tear of pain in the blackbird's eye. The bird cawed and flew off to the bridge. It perched on a lamppost and resumed staring at the guardian, his forgotten room, the Shell sign, and the *sidra* tree. Its eyes welled up in fear and pain. It cawed again and flew off toward Nahda Hospital. The guardian was terrified. He went inside and shut the door, annoyed that a passing bird was able to trap him inside his room.

s

In his sleep, he saw faces that chased him and tongues that taunted him. He saw barefoot crowds holding sticks and stones, screaming at him, "You lost the key to Muscat; you lost our country!" He recognized the faces of people he'd turned away from Muscat after they refused to give him something in return.

The crowds continued to demand that he open the gate. He screamed at them, "The key is lost! I don't know who stole it." The faces he recognized were a mix of those he'd seen as a guardian but never approached and those he saw when he left his forgotten room. He was surprised that the faces continued to chase and taunt him even though the gate was wide open.

He woke up suffocated by the sounds he'd heard in the dream. He realized he had no key, no gate, no life. A strange heaviness weighed down his chest. He opened the door and saw cars driving by. A cemetery had come up to confuse and besiege his memory, a cemetery for children. He thought of his children when he'd been alive, not knowing if they remembered him now, or if they'd consigned him to oblivion. He remembered how lovingly they'd greet him when he returned home each day after dusk. What was a children's cemetery doing here? Do the dead children dream of swinging across the bridge to cross over to the other side? Do they like the colors of the cars zooming by?

To insult the guardian's history and service to Muscat even more, Shell had put up a sign by his room. Behind the room now stood a bakery for hungry pedestrians. He thought, "What am I doing here on a Muscat night? I have no gate, no memory, no life, no food."

After much hesitation and fear, he opened the door. He saw shining lights. He was terrified by the sounds and lights, dazzled by the cars that zoomed by. He saw people streaming out of a nearby mosque, others from the bakery, yet others looking out from the balconies of their Wadi Hattat apartments. He couldn't understand anything. So he held tight to the trunk of the *sidra* tree.

"Where to, old man?" a taxi driver shouted at him.

S

Silently, he climbed the three steps up to his room and leaned against a lonesome wall. He remembered the sweltering days, the sick faces at Dr. Thoms's hospital.[1] How many patients had died because of the gate's strict opening hours and Muscat's fear of its children? He remembered the scent of lemons from faraway villages. Now, he saw nothing but asphalt and lights, a life without life, a bridge suspended under the sky.

He looked at the cars parked behind his room. Curiosity overcame him. He walked to the back and leaned against the wall. He saw cars refueling at the Shell station and the huge Wadi Hattat building. Snatches of a song drifted toward him from a nearby car. He didn't know which car or recognize the lyrics; only the word *door* struck him:

> A door that smells of jasmine,
> Door of sorrow, door of yen,
> A forlorn door, its people forgotten:
> This earth is full of homes.
> Lord, adorn them with doors,
> With no sorrow, no closed door.

He lost himself in the song. A tear rolled down his cheek as he stood, alone, leaning against the wall. He couldn't bear his burning tear. He decided to return to the room to bury his tears, alienation, and hunger. When he turned around, he saw policemen approaching. He was afraid that if he went inside, they would lock him up in his forgotten room. So he returned to the rear and sat down with his back against the wall. People went in and out of the bakery that had abandoned him in his hunger. The Shell station was still servicing cars. Indian families were celebrating on the balconies of the Wadi Hattat building. He didn't know when he slept. When he awoke at dawn, he found no bakery, mosque, station, or bridge. Muscat's gate was closed to him.

At five in the morning, two policemen found a man in a hospital gown lying under the bridge. One said to the other, "He must have escaped from Nahda Hospital." No water flowed under the bridge; no fish awaited the sunrise. The body of the man who'd guarded Muscat's gate in his youth lay by a forgotten room, under a *sidra* tree that birds had fled long ago.

Post Office of the Dead

There's no meaning in words that emerge from night-mares, nor in the emotions of a woman who's never plumbed the depths of nostalgia. There's no beauty in the thoughts of a poet who's never wrapped himself in anxiety and isolation, nor in the passage of time that hasn't wounded a human soul. The shade of a tree unbowed by drought has no meaning.

You sit alone in a small café opposite Al Amerat's post office, stringing together words to capture last night's terrors, cloaking the woman and the road and the shadow in a story. You don't wait for letters, poems, or friends, nor do you ponder a passerby's laughter or remember the dead man you wanted to write about, although you don't know what killed him. Facing you is a small forest of concrete created by a distorted modernity, with milling workers oppressed by a scorching summer and the hunger of exile. In the concrete forest, you see bodies exposing their anxiety on balconies that overlook only boredom, emptiness, and black streets. On one of the balconies, a woman hangs up the day's wash, while a child chases sunbeams with his water gun. A man on another balcony inscribes on a sheet of white paper the long list of his debts, which have grown steadily since the oil company fired him, debts that want to shove him off his balcony into a prison cell. The white paper turns red.

The post office stands alone, without a single tree for company. Where will the birds land, burdened with messages from the dead, foreigners, lovers, thieves, and prisoners? Several school buses are parked near the lonely post office's white wall, left to broil in the summer sun after the drivers left for their childhood villages, while the students forgot laughter, worries, and the words of the national anthem under the seats.

s

What if, breaking all barriers between time and space, imagination and reality, a letter from Fyodor Dostoyevsky arrived at Al Amerat's post office? Dostoyevsky from Russian soil and a letter written in the imagination of a man sitting in a café across from the post office will disrupt a poor postmaster's life. That's what I thought when I saw the postmaster enter his office.

The letter that appeared on his desk later that day read:

To Anna Grigoryevna:
Moscow / May 25, 1880

My gentle angel, dove of my soul, Anya my love:
    Yesterday I arrived in Moscow. Tomorrow Pushkin's statue will be unveiled. I'll give a speech to extol our great poet, although I don't know which

newspaper will publish it. It doesn't matter. The important thing is that many Russian newspapers will publish my speech and many of my enemies and friends will be present.

Last night I sent off the last section of *The Brothers Karamazov.* I haven't had any epileptic seizures recently, which is good. The weather promises rain and a difficult winter. I'm very happy, Anya, that I'll finally be rid of the vile, thieving publishers who've been sucking my blood like mosquitoes for the last ten years. I'll devote myself to writing the book I've been dreaming about, without the nightmare of debts and creditors.

I'm very busy and in an ungodly rush. Tomorrow morning, I have several engagements. I hope this message finds you in good health. Hug the little ones for me warmly and with great affection.

What will the postmaster, who's been bored of his job for years, do after receiving Dostoyevsky's letter? What if I walked into his office and asked him for it? He would reply in confusion, "How do you know this man from a faraway country?"

"My brother, I've been waiting for this letter for a year."

"Wait, let me ask my boss. He's traveling right now. Check back with us later."

He sent a WhatsApp message to his boss, who was vacationing overseas, asking him what to do about a letter lost in time that had vanished from the memory of people and governments and somehow landed in his forgotten post office.

I saw the rising anxiety and terror on his face. He took the letter, looked closely at the sender's name, tried to spell it out, became frustrated, opened the drawer of his desk, and put the letter away. The imaginary letter lay alone in the postmaster's drawer in Al Amerat, while Dostoyevsky's wife waited anxiously for it to bring news of her husband. She feared he'd had another seizure. Unease began to gnaw on the postmaster's mind. He walked out to the lobby, thinking about the man who'd asked for the letter. Perhaps he'd been sent by the higher-ups to monitor my work. He didn't look like he was from Al Amerat, and his accent seemed odd. Could this be a joke by one of my friends? My life really can't bear any jokes!

He reconsidered the first possibility, that the higher-ups were testing him. But why, at a post office where there's no work, hardly any letters? It's a busy week for me if a single letter shows up.

"They can watch me all they want, not like there are any promotions or bonuses," he told himself huffily, foreclosing this possibility.

That night, he searched for the man named Dostoyevsky. Google turned up a photo of a man with a long beard. What does he want from a forgotten post office? He read some cursory facts: Russian, wrote novels, imprisoned and sick, in debt his whole life. He tried to connect all this information about a bearded man who'd been dead for more than a century and a half, but he couldn't find any link to Al Amerat.

"Naturally, a man who's turned to dust and who spent his life in debt wouldn't want to live in a roomless post office without trees," the postmaster said to himself.

He found the second possibility—that the letter was a prank by one of his friends—to be more likely. He debated which of his friends might be responsible.

"I know them all. Nobody has any interest in books," he thought.

s

Another idea occurred to me for bringing drama to the forgotten post office that received no letters and giving nightmares to the postmaster, who'd never had a stressful day in his professional life. Perhaps, in his anxiety and fear, he'd ask his boss to cut his vacation short and return immediately.

That night, I imitated Franz Kafka's style to write a letter about Al Amerat.

To Max Brod
June 5, 1920

Dearest Max,

Have you heard about this city? I doubt it, although I sincerely hope you don't meet Azrael here, in this riverless city without a single proper café, bar, library, or museum, whose heat can melt your bones as you walk. It's guarded by mountains that never tire of staring at you, making you fear that they might assault you at any moment, as if there were a historical, religious, and psychological enmity between you and them, or as if you were a murderer and your victims were glaring balefully at you.

These guards are like soldiers returned from a lost war, so don't expect to find a single green tree in these mountains. Yesterday, I had a high fever. I looked around for a clinic but found nothing, not even a witch doctor, so I fell asleep in exhaustion in one of the abandoned school buses near the post office. Those buses were made in India. It's natural, Max, that you'll figure out that this city is close to India. I know how diligent you were at geography. I hope this letter finds you in good health. Please remember to go by my apartment once in a while, and don't neglect the plants on the balcony.

No doubt you're wondering how I got here. Yesterday, when I was burning up, I became delusional and saw myself in a city of the East. I apologize, this isn't really a city. We insult all the cities of the world and Ibn Khaldun—please don't ask me about Ibn Khaldun; it's not necessary to know everything—by calling this place a city.

You'll certainly find nothing here to make you happy. So, Max, if I die in this "city," please don't leave my body here. I don't want to be incinerated twice, once in life and again in Al Amerat's cemetery. I hope that you'll take my body, by any means possible, to Jerusalem or Prague. Please burn this letter so that no one remembers this city.

What will the postmaster do with Kafka's letter? Will he know how to pronounce the name? Will he wonder who "Max" is? He certainly knows the Max department stores in Muscat that sell clothes and peddle dreams with capitalist brands. This time he'll definitely contact the postmaster general.

Will he be confused and not finish the chess game he'd been playing on his phone? Although he usually loses to the chess app, today he'd captured a knight and two pawns.

The postmaster whispered to himself in the euphoria of victory, "The time of defeat is over, king." Before moving a pawn, he pondered one of his rooks, staring contemplatively at the black and white squares on the screen. Then he looked up and saw the two letters. Instantly, his euphoria gave way to anxiety. "What am I supposed to do with these letters with the postmaster general out of the country?" he thought.

He said bitterly to himself, "The bosses are off enjoying the cool, leaving us to roast in the *gharbī*."[1]

In these tense and anxious moments, the opponent's pawns attacked ruthlessly and cornered his king. He turned off the phone, saying to himself in frustration, "Even in games we lose."

When he turned on his phone the next morning to look up the man called Kafka, his terror increased. A youth with big ears and terrifying eyes appeared on the screen. He read about the frightened young man, learning that he was from eastern Europe, suffered from nightmares, and wrote stories and novels.

"As if the indebted Russian shepherd wasn't enough, now the shepherd of nightmares has also come for me," he thought.

Two hours passed as he continued to stare at the two letters. It was one o'clock in the afternoon. What should I do? The postmaster general won't respond to my messages.

The night before he'd dreamed of a man with a long beard lying on the floor of a dark cell, with a trickle of blood flowing from his mouth. The man on the cell floor was looking straight at him, pleading silently for help. He'd woken up, terrified by the pain radiating from the man's eyes.

On the way to the post office, he remembered that the man in his dream looked like the man called Dostoyevsky, whose picture he'd seen on his phone.

He thought of various schemes to unveil the trickster behind the prank. Then he hesitated, remembering the first possibility. What if these letters are a trap set by the higher-ups? Why are they testing me? I don't work at the White House! I've been doing this job for twenty-five years: tiny office, papers, boredom, air conditioner, some customers, occasional gossip.

He picked up his phone, went into the neighborhood group chat, and typed, "Guys who sent a letter to the post office: the Russian response is here." Minutes later, sarcastic replies flooded his screen, increasing his anxiety.

"Your brain's buried in Russia."

"Are you high or dreaming?"

"Get a real job, man!"

A variety of angry, smiling, surprised, dancing, and indecent emojis appeared, together with several insults.

After reading the replies, he was disappointed that his second theory for the two letters was also incorrect.

s

Here's the postmaster now, leaving his post office, checking the pocket of his white *dishdasha* and adjusting his turban to reveal a bald head before blowing his nose. Here he is looking at the café. I see him now, stroking his close-cropped salt-and-pepper beard, searching for the person behind the prank. From the café window, I look at the postmaster's face: anxious, fearful, distracted, devoid of life. We're separated by a street, glass, and the narrator's imagination. What if I invited him for a drink? No—I don't want to interfere. The postmaster just stood there, watching the street, shops, and passing cars. What if he crossed the street, came inside the café, peeped at my screen, and saw his anxiety written on the white page? But he didn't move, leaning against an abandoned school bus by the post office. He gazed at the Iranian fruit seller's shop, the tobacconist, and the Egyptian restaurant. He didn't notice anyone watching him. Beads of perspiration dripped down his face. Again, he stroked his beard, which the river of time was slowly washing into whiteness.

The Third Morning

In his early years at the post office, the postmaster would rifle voyeuristically through the letters of lovers and the worries of foreigners. Through his surreptitious reading, he knew about apartment rents and car payments and women's pregnancies that they wrote about to their mothers.

On this night, he recalled the full sweep of his professional life, seeing that he'd been swept away by age and time without realizing it until this moment. He remembered how he would open sealed letters without his boss or colleagues ever noticing.

"Perhaps I'm nearing the end of my career," he whispered to himself.

That night, I wrote fictitious names on several envelopes, filled them with flour and salt, and licked them shut.

"It's your last day, postmaster of a forgotten post office."

Before he got to work, my letters were scattered in front of Al Amerat's post office. At eight in the morning, an ambulance and a police car with flashing lights showed up.

(A week after this incident, the paramedic from the ambulance—whom I'd met at the same café where I wrote this text—told me that the postmaster had been raving about Russian and eastern European writers, saying over and over again: "Informants have stolen the country and tortured us!" He mentioned various dates and recited romantic verses. The police closed the case they'd registered against an unknown person. A month later, the paramedic stopped coming to the café. The waiter told me he'd retired.)

Now, here I am, paying for my last coffee before leaving the café, Al Amerat, and this text.

Unimportant Footnote to the Text's Shadow

Two incidents occurred during the time this text was written. The first: In a shop opposite the café near the post office, a police car would stop every morning, investigating a case of theft. The police didn't notice the anxiety of the postmaster standing there, nor did they see who dropped the letters off at the post office, nor did they observe the man who'd written the letters.

The second incident: In another shop adjacent to the café, workers were relentlessly hammering and banging the walls, creating a din that could be heard for a mile. Dostoyevsky wasn't among them because the Siberian prison had been shut down.

Marginal Shadow of a Forgotten Text

Dear narrator,

I'm sending you this letter because I'm certain that you'll come back to the café like a killer returning to a crime scene. Apologies, I shouldn't call you a killer, but you yourself think that you've killed a postmaster with your words and your imagination. I hope that, as you read this letter, you'll look up at the top of the wall from where you sit to write. Do you see the camera there? Don't be nervous. Don't think that you're alone in the café and can end my life with words. No, my friend. The thing is, after the police saw the video footage from this camera, they read your text and found out exactly when you were at the café and how you enjoyed torturing me.

I get it. Like me and many others in our country, you don't have the money to travel. So you said to yourself, "Let's have fun with the poor postmaster." Even though you have nothing to do with the mail. Why, you don't even have a mailbox!

Indeed, as the paramedic told you (according to your lies, which I doubt very much), on the morning of the third day, I fainted. Not only because of the stress, anxiety, and nightmares you inflicted upon me. I, like everyone else, have life and family problems. There's no need to mention my personal concerns to a nosy person like you. That night I was exhausted and anxious. I didn't sleep at all. When I arrived at the post office and saw the scattered letters, I became extremely agitated, which increased my tension. But what really terrified me was that I saw those two men from your letters looking at me through a window. I can't say if I was hallucinating because of fatigue, or if I actually saw them. But there they were, staring right at me, the man with the long beard and the youth with the big ears.

Then I collapsed.

I found myself later that night in Nahda Hospital (perhaps your friend, the paramedic, told you about this). A week later, I emerged from a state of delirium. The police uncovered the truth, not for my sake, but because of your little arsenic hoax. They read everything on your computer.

I'd like you to know that I've filed for retirement. I don't want to get you in trouble with the courts for a text you wrote because you were bored. Or perhaps you don't like this city. It doesn't really matter. Now, dear narrator, won't you please invite me in for a cup of coffee? I'll tell you my real story at the forgotten post office, and you can tell me all about the two writers in whose names you wrote those letters.

I await your reply.

The Postmaster
Al Amerat

Who Stole Muscat's Noses?

Muscat doesn't love you and you don't love it. But neither does it hate you, nor do you hate it. You don't long for Muscat, while it doesn't yearn for foreigners and transients, or give too much thought to the expatriates in its neighborhoods. In the twilight, you can probe things impartially and in great depth, win games of chance, be like an anxious, sharp-eyed eagle observing fine and scattered details with the amazement of a child. Perhaps you *are* a child with the anxiety of an ancient eagle. Or maybe you're a broken crutch on potholed paths. The arduous road pushes you to explore its side streets and alleys with passion and eager anticipation, to inspect its details and shadows, to learn about its endings open to closed possibilities, to shut the windows overlooking the marginal.

There's no place for apprehension here, no room for sentimentality when the city's soul is moving and transforming, with guarantee of neither constancy nor change, no light at the beginning of the tunnel, or indeed any tunnels at all in which stray dogs can snooze during the day or street cats can slumber at night.

Muscat is surrounded by arid mountains and the ashes of stories, both confusing and perplexed, solid on the surface, shifting by night. It's immersed in its hurtful language and daily misery, besieged by its defeated history and the geography of chaos, by the chaos of details and the wall of fear, by doors that open in the morning for the hungry and shoeless to begin their exile. Its history is scattered across smuggling ships, historical archives, odes of betrayal, the rifles of invaders, and the fantasies of patriotic writers.

There's no time to explore Muscat's marginalized body or its shattered and marginal face, for time is stagnant here. Forgetfulness has erased Muscat's past, while its present is riddled with disappointments, even as its future is left to pirates and thieves. If it weren't for the languid movement of the shadow of a small tree atop Bawshar's mountains, I would have asserted that time hasn't passed here at all. Were it not for a street cleaner's song by Mutrah's fish market, I would have said that this city's heart is so devastated by sorrow that it doesn't love joy, as if afflicted by all of life's troubles.

Muscat clings to the blue of its waters and its imaginary, forgotten stories, huddling with its back against indifferent mountains like a blind old woman, continuing to postpone its eternally deferred dreams. Saltwater laps at its feet, although the salt has morphed into a desert and the Salty Desert neighborhood has become a colony of global capitalism. The salt forgot its desert, intent on watching the black liquid flowing to the port. The salt couldn't walk into the port to ask: Where's the country's oil going? Why is it fleeing the port along with the water?

A surly guard protecting the port yelled at the salt, "Who the hell do you think you are to come in here?"

The salt replied angrily, "Who am I? I'm the country's salt. You are its wound!"

Dejected, the salt returned to its desert, thinking of schemes to sneak into the port and satisfy its curiosity about where the oil was going and what the pirate ships were up to. After a while, it seeped into the pipelines passing over Salty Desert and made its way to a large duct beneath the guard's room. It paused for a moment, chuckling to hear the guard's loud snores as he slept, oblivious to the oil he was supposed to be protecting. The salt said to itself, "What do I want anyway from a country whose guards are asleep?"

The salt forgot about the sleeping guard. It continued on to the port, stopping to rest a little and look upon a huge ship smuggling away the country's oil and its history and its dreams. Atop the ship fluttered the flag of a nation over which the sun never sets, but whose ugliness rises every morning in all directions. Before returning to its desert, the salt recalled a blind cemetery custodian who used to sing to the dead. It laughed again, saying, "These guards are guarding the city's delusions and its dead."

The salt hung around for a while to watch the last few café patrons burying their nightly hunger. Then it went weeping to its desert, dissolved into the ground, and disappeared.

Since that day, the salt hasn't asked about Muscat, fearing for the city's wounded memory. The people of Muscat don't wonder about its story either, having forgotten all about the country's salt, alone in the desert.

S

Muscat isn't your hometown, nor is it your downfall. Muscat is Azzan bin Qais watching the bakery near his grave, then walking over to quarrel with a man sleeping in a mud hut under the bridge. Muscat is Fairuz's voice from a small balcony in Mutrah, singing:

> We can only count, so we count . . .
> The days.
> How we wasted our days!
> And dreams . . .
> Oh, how we nurtured our dreams!

You don't see who's behind the balcony or why he's counting the days, but you do realize what it means to lose your dreams in this city. Is there a widow up there, or a soldier fleeing war? Or perhaps a lover with a broken heart?

A little fish in a pool by Wadi Adai awaits a blind hunter, while the blind hunter waits for a spear made from the wood of a dead tree on a mountaintop. Drought awaits the mountain's creatures. Forlorn statues of horses at a roundabout await war, or someone to guide them to the children's park, or to Bawshar's mountains. The general stands on a mountain peak, not to track bored horses, but to look down over slumbering Muscat while smoking a Cuban cigar despite his hatred for Cuba. At the beach, a lover steals a kiss in the dark. Indian men at a tavern in Qurum discuss how to make even more profits at markets across the country. A man takes his 1999 Lexus to Wadi Kabir for repairs after being momentarily distracted by the corruption of oil pirates.

Fernando Pessoa is at Sira Fort trying to smuggle away the body of his murderous grandfather on a fishing boat before the coast guard can catch him. Meanwhile, Kafka sits in a café across from the Central Bank, waiting for six in the evening to look at ravens and a ticking clock that doesn't know its country's time. A poet up on the heights of illusion that he never descends tries to write about the nightmares that haunt his sleep, about pirates and their ships in whose decks he tries to hide.

In Arabic, *Muscat* means "place of falling." Indeed, things fall in this city every morning: dreams fall, words fall from newspapers, delusional people fall into the traps of light, nostalgia falls upon its ancient paths and in the voices of peddlers in the Neighborhood of the Blind, the smell of coffee falls into a cup or on a woman's mouth, birds and butterflies fall in Muscat's gardens, Muscat falls in the sketchbook of a young student drawing the sea and mountains guarding the sea and forts guarding the landscape and a flag atop a fort that he leaves uncolored, a rose falls on a lover's breast or in a blind poet's verse, failures fall in a dream, seats and soldiers and informants and saints and contradictions and sailors' curses sometimes fall from Muscat's sky, and half the story falls on the rotten half of the apple of a narrator contemplating a bird confused by the directions atop Sahwa Tower. Don't be surprised if a seat falls on you while you're walking, running, dreaming, or anxiously scratching your head. Expect any type of seat to fall: the seat of power, a poet's seat or a guard's, an old storyteller's seat, or even an inquisitor's. Muscat is quite generous with seats for foreigners, even, on occasion, murderers. *Falling* is both a noun and an adjective in Arabic, a perpetual extension of Muscat, in whose streets only boredom, nostalgia, and poverty can rise.

Can you rid yourself of your conscience in this city, whose own conscience is dead or hidden, murdered or betrayed? A city's conscience is probably a single unified entity, no matter how many tongues it might have. Or else it's neutral, without bias or favoritism. Do cities have living consciences? Maybe, maybe not, but they certainly have pulsating souls through which they perceive children's laughter, the joy of trees, and the anxiety of their streets. Even passersby know a city's soul, that which residents, lovers, madmen, and the poor all breathe. Poets can grasp a city's soul as it tries to flee the wolves of modernity, without hope of rescue. For now, let's leave aside the traps of language and its deceptive pronouns. Let's instead follow Muscat's scent, which needs a dog's nose or a lover's eye to sense it.

You can feel Muscat's soul, but it's like jelly, transparent, invisible, impossible to hold or describe. Sometimes it grows; sometimes it vanishes. Muscat itself is huge if you consider its wounds and dreams, but tiny in its present, and silent despite the words aging beyond its walls, walkways, and closed doors. It's expansive even with its suffocating spaces, tempting the imagination of poets and the pockets of thieves, driving away the country's tribes, seducing invaders and their greed.

So where's your soul, Muscat? Are your scents hidden in your street corners, or your thresholds, or perhaps under your bridges? How can we begin to search for your scents? Could it be that what leads us to the heart of your story or to your secret springs are the doves of Ruwi or Khuwair, or those asleep under Mirani Fort? (Those doves resemble the souls of people who died in the neighboring fort. At night, you can imagine birds asleep on the foothills. With the light of white buildings reflecting upon them, they resemble sheets forgotten by soldiers or missionaries who passed through Muscat, or the kisses of lovers tired of waiting for ships. Perhaps at dawn these birds imagine the souls of children abducted from distant villages and left at the fort, or the tears of their mothers, or the silent prayers that immigrants offer at the creek.) Can doves distract us from the madmen walking your streets? I don't know, but I don't see a madman in you, Muscat, or a spring, or a bird, or a poet uncovering meaning in your alleys and arguments.

So where do this city's madmen go? No matter. Let's leave them alone in their absence or presence, or in their darkness. Let's search instead for the city's lovers, in streets and alleys, under the trees perching on balconies, until we find the missing thread of the city's story. Will we find them on Love Street? Or on Mutrah's corniche? Or perhaps by a tree near Seeb's fish market? Let's try looking for Muscat's scent on the shores of Qurayyat, in the story of a fisherman who returned from exile in the early seventies, or let's try the other side of Muscat, by the chimneys of Rusail's factories that inflame noses and fumigate the capital every morning. Or have people's noses completely lost their sense of smell?

Have people become infected with some strange disease so they can't smell their city's scents? Or were their noses stolen? Did something damage their souls, making them lose their grip on the city?

Muscat's people know its scent, but they have no idea who stole it, or stole their noses. Perhaps they knew once, long ago, but were too afraid to speak the truth. Some of them still know Muscat by heart, even after a defective life has robbed them of their city's scent.

s

Muscat is both dawn and noon; it's night and the darkness in a blind man's eyes and the light in a story; Muscat is shadows falling upon paths and trees shading streets; it's the birds of morning and the seagulls of Mutrah. Muscat is boredom and lovers' tales; it's the executioner's laugh and the martyr's tears; Muscat is time and thirst and the dreams of those crushed by the illusions of modernity; it's hunger past, renewed, and future; Muscat is the sea's neglect of a port and the port's fear of invaders and pirates and their ships; it's the crying of children abducted from faraway villages and forests, and also the laughter of children playing in Riyam Park. Muscat is the wonder in the eyes of a child from a mountain village when he sees the sea for the very first time; it's the trumpet's honk when the flag is lowered at seven in the evening and the drum's beat when the flag is raised at seven in the morning. Muscat is time and no-time, or times hidden, fabricated, or lost in the fragility of memory, and in the deceit of history.

Muscat at dawn is a donkey eating patchy grass by the roadside, a dog languidly extending its paws by a fisherman's café near Mutrah's Fish roundabout, another one playing with crows in a backyard, and a third dog chasing the dreams of poets. It's a dove watching a young Indian woman through an apartment window as she plays soft temple music, a mouse haunting the imagination of a poet who's spent all night at the tavern. Muscat is a cat in a lover's embrace by the sea, a sea forbidden to those without tickets to travel, a port speaking the languages of India, a man who whiles away his days in the playground of memories.

Muscat's time rides upon its weary back to seep into the dreams of passersby, bent by the tales of history, by the hunger of fishmongers in the markets and on the sidewalks, by the fish of its seas smuggled to distant countries, by the dream chasers of its deserts, by the worshippers of its deformed modernity, and by the seekers of its hidden charms. Muscat's time passes heavily and slowly and stickily over details, sometimes stopping altogether, abandoning the city to hurtle toward its imagination, to its hunger for death, to the embrace of invaders, to the stories of hunters and the songs of shepherds beyond its walls. Muscat frees itself from the time of man, yearning for hidden joys and a passion for exodus, rendering its inhabitants timeless. Or perhaps time itself tires of Muscat and its people, fleeing on a boat, or an oil tanker, or upon the feathers of a bird flying off to faraway continents.

You see Muscat's people searching for their time and the time of their city like madmen, as if they were searching for a corpse in the mountains at night. In this search, they fall into many traps. Alienation tears them apart and consumes their joy, while anxiety sucks the wonder out of their souls. They yearn for beginnings, for Muscat's silence at night, for its bright stars, for the wells that used to quench their thirst on the outskirts of Ruwi.

Have you ever seen city dwellers chasing time? They gather by the sea to try to catch the fish of an idyllic past, but instead the whale of a predatory present assails them, devouring their joy, their voices, their memories, so that, ultimately, they fall victim to the maw of a ravenous future.

What tempts you to write about this enigmatic city, simple yet complex, clear yet scandalous, gazing longingly upon the carnival of distorted modernity? One of its feet is in the sea, the other planted rigidly atop the mountains, like a child tied to the trunk of a dead tree, dreaming of travel to faraway lands.

This city opens its heart to the Indian Ocean, so India comes here with its people and its culture, its smells and its spices, with sidewalk spittle and songs that seep from shanty huts and films that play at Ruwi's cinema every evening. India leaks into Ruwi and Darsait; into temples and churches; into kitchens, factories, and markets; into the country's veins. The Indian wave won't stop at Darsait's roundabout, but will seep into the country's life, its trade and markets and the tongues of its people.

You must find a bored taxi driver to guide you to Muscat's hidden stories, or look for a fishmonger, or a shepherd who left his mountains, or a fisherman who forgot his boat, or a retired prison guard to tell you about Muscat's scent and its ordinary people. Why confuse the reader with Muscat's scent? What if Muscat was without scent, timeless, soulless? Do we have to make up a scent for it, burden it with time, implant a soul in its street like roses? All cities give birth to themselves in moments of defeat or victory, after which people turn to them like widows returning from war.

s

Muscat is woodcutters without firewood or forest, water carriers without water or *falaj* in a time of thirst, wars with new and deadly killers, deserted neighborhoods, forts abandoned by invaders for other invaders, the cameras of tourists, the sea's solitude, and dates that escaped from the textbooks of history. It's filled with the smells and tears and memories of the blind. Muscat is starving bodies asleep at the governor's gate, a gate separating two times, unrelated to the symbolism of doors, neither wooden nor iron, not protecting invaders, but rather imprisoning the country within itself. After half a century, we'll realize that this city's time is one: its hunger is one, its dreams are one, its fear is renewed, its lovers are many, its thieves are even more plentiful, and its disappointments multiply every dawn. The governor's door remains up-right like a proud, lonely *alif*, leading nowhere, not shed-ding the blood of the city's stories.

Muscat is shepherds and shame, sprawling even as it shrinks from fatigue, attracting rural dreams, repelling even the idea of the word *city* as it searches for its lost voice. Its original inhabitants are afraid of their own shad-ows, worried about the crowds flocking to their memo-ries, fearful of the concrete forests that engulf them. The newcomers, in contrast, are amazed by concrete, but also more worried, having left behind the shadows of their childhoods in distant villages, which no longer accom-modate their anxiety and longing, even as Muscat is no longer the wonder of their dreams, for it doesn't recognize the smells of their childhood or the songs of their youth. Strangers to the countryside, anxious in the city, they plant their feet in their ancestral villages, even as their hearts remain in Muscat.

Muscat watches the anxiety of its original inhabitants and newcomers alike, trying carefully despite its own fa-tigue to dampen their rising fear every night, even as oc-casional moments of fusion or fragmentation bring the two groups together.

s

Muscat is lame, attractive yet barren, a flower aban-doned to memory by shepherds, travelers, and beggars, ignored by all except the sea. Only the sea continues to cling to Muscat's memory and its tears, although it, too, is merciless, throwing invaders onto the city's shores and providing easy passage to the ships of oil thieves. From the mountains, woodcutters will carry firewood to the markets, as fishermen cast their nets into the sea at night. At dawn the market will burn down and the fishermen will starve. Famine will loom in the faces of Muscat's people, as it has from the beginning.

Oh, how many doors you have, Muscat, and how few windows, but isn't a single sea-facing window enough for you to look out over your wounds and your dreams?

Shadows of Muscat's Fragile Heart

Kareena Kapoor stands atop the Bridge Hotel, staring vacantly at pedestrians on the eponymous bridge. The Bollywood screen goddess doesn't pay much attention to passersby, studying instead her own image and smile withering under Ruwi's sun. She considers the makeup on her face, the redness of her lips, the whiteness of her teeth, and her sun-bleached hair. She thinks about the gold that will relocate to her country at the end of the year and about her contract that will be renewed next year. What if Kareena stepped out of the billboard and out of time and walked over to the fields to hear farmers' stories and smell Ruwi's soil? What if she sang for her countrymen at Ruwi's cinema? What if she stared at the billboard next to hers and saw the Omani girl holding a basket of imported fruit in her hand? What if Kareena asked for a red apple, not to escape the deceptive image, but to become its Scheherazade? Perhaps the two would strike up a conversation, the girl with the fruit basket asking Kareena about her childhood and her country and her lovers.

Kareena returns to her billboard at the end of the night. What if she were to leave her country, saying, "I want to die here, in Oman"? What if she walked to the nearby Indian restaurant to order a scorchingly spicy meal? What if she looked east and saw the Alawiyah mosque's minaret and wondered about its architectural style?

But the billboard atop Bridge Hotel came down at the end of the year, before Kareena's dreams could come true, before she could renew her contract, and before her makeup melted under the blazing Ruwi sun.

Kareena Kapoor returned to her country, and the Bridge Hotel continued to watch pedestrians crossing the bridge, feeling a gnawing sense of weariness. The bridge, too, felt weary and lonesome after municipal workers took down the billboard of the Indian actress. For years, street cleaners have been gazing longingly up at the Bridge Hotel, asking, "When will Kareena come back?"

The Blind Water Carrier

He was a child in Ruwi, helping his father, who worked as a guard at the governor's gate by night and a water seller by day during a time of thirst. Thirst and hunger killed his father in Ruwi. The child knew Muscat's paths and lanes like the back of his hand. He carried water upon his little head to distant homes, sometimes sitting under a shady tree to wait for the neighborhood girls to buy his water. Together, they would sing songs whose meaning he didn't understand, their heads full of morning scents and the dreams of life.

He couldn't recall when the darkness came upon him, but he remembered Ruwi's neighborhoods and farms. He remembered his father's tent and his funeral. At the age of ten, he'd learned the language of the Banyans,[1] humming songs in that foreign tongue. He remembered the mornings, the heat, the scents. He knew the secrets of homes, the stories of lovers and immigrants, of people dreaming about passports to escape Muscat and its hunger. Huddling in the tent with his mother, he listened to stories about his father, about their village tucked between the mountains.

He said to his mother, "We should go back to our village."

She told him, "We'd be even hungrier there."

The child went on selling water, learning languages, and quarreling with girls on the street, while hunger and the girls' songs continued to haunt his dreams, as they do today, in the autumn of his life.

The Blind Man's Final Gesture

"Where does the darkness lead you, blind man?"

"It leads me to the first springs of wonder, to the soul's roots."

"But you don't see the springs."

"I don't see the springs, yet I bathe in them every night."

Trees of Ash

In a dream I saw trees that resembled children's laughter, the tears of widows, and the wisdom of my ancestors. By morning the trees had burned down to ash, all except one, which continued to haunt me every night: a woman's tree that wouldn't catch fire but kept its distance.

> A tree dies and stays, scattered throughout Nature.
> A flower withers and its dust endures forever.
> A river runs and flows into the sea and its water will
>   always be what was its.
> I pass and I stay, like the Universe.
>   —Fernando Pessoa, "The Keeper of Flocks"[1]

A tree in your yard is the soul of a woman of your lineage. So preserve your lineage's soul with water and love.

1

Whenever I see a lonely tree up on a mountain, or in the distance, or even on a street corner, I think of poetry, mothers, Abbas Kiarostami, and my distant childhood.[2]

2

Have you ever looked at ashes scattered around a fireplace at night and recalled the loneliness of a tree? Did the smell of smoke from a smoldering palm tree on the outskirts of your village ever seep into your nose on a winter morning, making you miss your childhood and shed a single nostalgic tear? Have you ever carried a bundle of firewood on your head while worrying about life and death? Do you yearn for the trees in your backyard when you're far from home? Has your soul hugged a lonesome tree in the desert as you pondered the earth's loss and the sorrow of forests? Have you ever scattered tree ashes in the fields and perceived the circle of time and life?

If your answer to these questions is yes, then you're a lover of the spirit of trees; in fact, you're one of its righteous children. If your answer is no, then this text isn't for you.

3

I recollect a phrase from an Omani novel: we were all trees once, but only some of us remained loyal to our roots.

Wouldn't it be nice if, just like trees, people were devoted to benevolence and charity? The tree teaches man the meaning of giving, revelation, and renunciation. It's a master of resisting drought, death, rejection, and ugliness, symbolizing only goodness and generosity. When we want to describe a generous person, we say, "Your hand is green." Or we tell a kindhearted person, "Your soul is green."

Much can be written about the tree, its myriad interpretations, contents, branches, and roots clinging to the soil of meaning and the depth of metaphor, with all the connotations of transformation and rootedness. But I don't want writing about trees to be incoherent or scattered, for a simple and fundamental reason: I want to learn from trees the meaning of progress, commitment, and patience. To put it simply, I want to be a student at the School of Trees.

Those trees dotting the slopes at dawn are women waiting for their lovers who'll never return from their eternal absence.

4

The tree is a true and eternal mother to man, beast, and all beings: the mother of beginnings and endings. It's the apple of our father Adam, the final stop for souls at the farthest boundary in the seventh heaven,[3] and Noah's ark in the flood. The tree is your home, the bird's nest, the immigrant's abode, and the traveler's refuge on a blistering summer afternoon. It's the childhood you spent among date palms, or your memory shading the details of yearning, or a flowing spring on the banks of your daily nostalgia.

The tree is a seafarer's shoe, a ladder for ascending to the heavens of meditation, a train escaping the boredom and cruelty of cities, a carriage drawn by time and imagination along the roads of memory, the throat of a songbird or shepherdess, a silent spirit that speaks to whoever listens to it or trains his soul to perceive shadows and margins, daughter of water and mud, friend to the sun and dawn and birds, a kind teacher who adores the wind.

5

Along the roadside stood a single tree growing between tall, aloof buildings. A woman standing nearby said to me, "Take a branch and plant it in your heart. You'll never taste loss again."

Then she walked up to the tree and broke off a small branch. Before I left, the tree whispered to me, "Never plant anything in your heart except longing. Remember that a woman will always sow eternal yearning in your soul."

Before the sun set that day, I stood under the tree, picked a yellow flower, and planted it on the grave of a woman who'd slipped away into eternal absence.

6

You want to write about your first tree, or about the trees that embraced you in moments of fear, joy, or hunger, or about the ones that hurt you. You remember from your childhood a small farm next to your grandfather's lonely room, surrounded by palms, quince, and lemon trees. From the shade of those trees, you came to understand scents and shadows, not as a mere game, but as life itself.

That first tree encouraged me in my initial moments and steps, letting me play in its shade and teaching me to recognize the deception of light and the nobility of shadows. From those childhood shadows, I learned the true nature of my orphanhood, stretching from the river of time to the mountains of life.

Not far from his lonely room, during a time of drought and migration, a grandfather dug a well and planted a tree next to it. He passed away, but the tree remained, standing alone, preserving the memory of drought and the blind grandfather's foresight. A naughty, dreamy, and imaginative grandchild will climb the tree to chase his dream, but he'll fall from a high branch. From that fall he'll learn the first of life's lessons: never stop trying.

7

My friend, we love trees because they're like us but far more beautiful, purer, nobler, more compassionate, loyal to places, steadfast in times of change, changing in times of stagnation, resolute in the face of drought and death, swaying with wind and water and human greed and the hunger of birds, dancing with raindrops, listening to the breeze's prayers, clinging to the earth, quarreling with the sky, pondering the movements of stars and meteors, extending their roots into the hearts of mountains and deserts and plateaus and the earth's arteries, scattering their offspring over long distances across cities and villages and forests and riverbanks, measuring time and the changing of seasons with their shadows, capturing the cruelty of death, getting drunk on the music of birds at dawn, giving man everything and asking for nothing in return but love. But this brutal, savage creature has murdered hundreds of tree tribes and races, destroying entire forests just to don the ugly cloak of civilization. Perhaps I'm wrong to refer to tribes and races. For the tree is one and the same, with no tribes to separate it or races to disperse it, singular in its love, unique in its eternal nobility.

So yes, trees are like us, but we can't even begin to approach their characteristics or the essence of their meaning. The tree is a house, a window, a door, a road, a travel companion, a child's bed, a coffin, a stretcher to carry the wounded toward death or salvation. The tree gives you joy, grants you fragrance, gifts you meaning and lessons, opens the door to dawn with its scent. It's a good teacher, but also a faithful student of the sun, patience, water, travelers, and charity.

The tree doesn't fight the wind, but holds dialogue with it; it doesn't hate drought, but befriends it, deceiving it into forgetfulness; it doesn't begrudge the man who cuts it down, but gives him a lesson in endeavor and renewal. Will man learn from the tree the meaning of dialogue instead of war, hatred, and malice for anyone who disagrees with him? The tree doesn't humiliate itself in the face of drought, choosing instead to die standing proud and tall, without suffering or screaming, departing this realm with the dignified silence of nobility and greatness.

The tree doesn't claim wisdom or knowledge, nor does it boast of its mastery, as it scales the walls of houses, cemeteries, gardens, prisons, and balconies to share its insights with the sun. You must approach it, not with a student's passion, nor the quiet yearning of the wise, nor the naïveté of the lofty, nor the arrogance of the hasty, nor the ugliness of braggarts. Seeker of wisdom, you must open the windows of your soul to the tree's sanctity before approaching it, not with the intention of begging for a life lesson, but for love, for the first lesson you learn from a tree is that there is no communion between beings, no knowledge of the other, without love.

My friend, have you ever seen a lonely tree high in the mountains, or on a deserted road? That's a special type of tree, a poet reciting his verse to the sky, and to passersby and the departed.

8

Trees feed you, give you shade, wash away your heart's fatigue from the aridity of life, illuminate the night for seekers of warmth and light, shelter your grave from the harsh sun, and lead you to your homeland, or to your exile.

We mustn't forget that the tree can also be the handle of the ax that cuts down mothers, the spear that pierces bodies in battle, the firewood that feeds the inferno of hatred. Such a tree will whisper to you kindly and with great tenderness, "Forgive me. I only meant to do good, but man snatched away my bones and put them in the spears of evil and arrows of hatred that he made for his brothers and enemies."

No one knows a tree's secret except a passerby or a hungry bird.

9

From bookshelves lined with novels to the paper on which wills, poems, and death sentences are written, from a seed to the branch and the bird's nest, to the shepherd's staff and the Sufi's reed flute, to the warrior's spear and the blind man's stick, to a cottage's thatched roof and a fisherman's hut, to a bridge over the river and the throne under a king, to the wood coffin that carries us on the last journey, the tree undergoes countless transformations, asserting its overwhelming and aesthetic presence in myriad details, in life and death, and in absence.

The forest is dry,
The woodcutter is blind,
The ax gleams in the distance, and in dreams.
So why don't fires break out?

10
The Memory of Trees

The Gas Station Tree

On your way to Ruwi or Mutrah, as you cross Hamriyah Bridge, you see on your left a Shell gas station, over which sprouts a lonely green tree, growing above an ugly block of concrete, extending its roots, not to the black liquid, but to its friend, clear water in a white tank. The tree doesn't scream at passersby, but rather gives a lesson to those searching for the meaning of life and resistance, while gifting poets material for a mournful metaphor: a tree at a station for petrol extracted from the blood of its ancestors. You, the poet searching for meaning, must ask the wind about the gas station tree's first seed.

The Roundabout Tree

It stands like a mother welcoming her returning children, but they're in too much of a rush to pay attention, busy like pupils on the first day of school. The tree stands alone, welcoming travelers, crying over their deaths. It's a sign, not only for passersby and travelers, but one distinguishing life from death. Like a woman of exquisite beauty, this *ghāf* tree stands tall and proud, watching the statues of hungry horses on the roundabout. It welcomes visitors to Al Amerat with a lover's joy and bids them farewell with a widow's sadness.

The ʿAlʿalān of the Green Mountain

Up on the heights the *ʿalʿalān* clings to its roots,[4] chants the hymn of eternity with the wind, watches the clouds, sings to the stars, perfumes the paths with the fragrance of its soul. In its memories are words and stories and the smell of blood and dreams, while tucked away in its branches are long-forgotten songs. Sometimes it misses its friend the *ʿitma*,[5] which went off to a nearby village to become a roof for a home or mosque, or firewood for the winter stove and its stories. The *ʿalʿalān*'s scent perfumes worshippers on their way to the dawn prayer.

The School Sidra

The *sidra* was my fifth grade girlfriend, standing in a schoolyard corner, watching our rowdiness and laughing at our fear of the teacher's cane. It would look upon the ships we sketched in our notebooks during art class, surprised that village children who'd never seen blue waters could draw the sea. It used to say, "As long as the ships are wooden, they come from me." I would sit at the desk closest to the window, so whenever I got bored of the teacher's droning lecture, I could watch birds dancing in its branches. Although I felt close to the tree's shadow as it moved along the wall, it remained distant, busily re-arranging the students' dreams.

The Sarḥa of the Cemetery

It stood in desolation, swaddling the dead's loneliness. I'd known it since childhood, perhaps as well as I knew my own face. We carried the child who'd left life early and laid him to rest under it. The *sarḥa* shaded my brother's grave, watching over him with the tenderness of a woman who'd never had a child but considered all children to be her own. At night, the cemetery's children would rise to give water to their mother. The *sarḥa* hasn't withered in thirty years, guarding the cemetery, carrying the souls of the dead, with a secret in its name and comfort for those sleeping beneath.

s

Trees are diverse and intricate: trees of texts and trees of thieves, trees for cemeteries and trees for the gardens of modernity, a tree for family and another for life, a tree on the blouse of a woman speeding along a winding road to the forest, trees for the whiteness of snow and trees for the loneliness of the desert, a *ghāf* tree under which coffee and its story come to life, trees of home and childhood, trees guarding orphaned mountains, trees that shade meaning in the Empty Quarter, trees preserving an ancient folktale about the mountain's love for the sea, a tree upon which a raven builds its poem, trees on the apartment balconies of foreigners, a tree in the hand of a blind man asleep in the forest of old age, trees high up on the mountains guarding the magic of the stars.

11

A table at a café said to the poet, "I am a daughter of the forest, but I abandoned my mother far away, leaving my blood on the woodcutter's hand. So listen to the sound of migratory birds in my memory."

12

Whenever the general shot an arrow toward life, the Sufi's reed flute shouted in his face. Every time the fisherman speared a lake fish, another tree sprouted in the bard's poem.

13

Upon the tree perch the birds of speech and metaphor; from the tree sprouts life, and death descends.

The tree is speech, a lit window, a house door, a guard's companion, a teacher's cane, a student's toy, the crutch of time, the dancer's seductiveness, the poet's chair, a coffin for the dead, the body of a footbridge, the ashes of shepherds, and coffee served at a temple. We hung our childhood on a tree before heading off to the spring to fish for stories. But when we tried to return to the tree and our childhood, we found nothing but the wind, eternity, and the tears of our mothers.

From the tree fly the birds of speech and metaphor.

14

Whoever goes to a tree with the passion of a child will return with poems in his heart and the path to the divine stretching out in front of him. Whoever yearns for his ancestors or plants a tree in his yard will be missed by all of the earth's forests. The tree isn't a way to the forest, but rather a path toward the fragility of things. Or it's the forgotten first kiss that the sun planted upon the body of the earth.

15

Strangers are forgotten trees along walking paths.

16

In plains of sight, are you rapt in watching o tree?
As with a thousand strings you with the life of
    mankind
are bound,
do not fear thunder,
do not fear lightning for you stand strong, o tree.
Raise your head o you who are fretful, for like our
    hope,
you are with us o you singular yet alone o tree.
        —Siavash Kasrai, "Ode to a Tree"[6]

Music

Music, my friend, is the salt of speech and its sugar, life flowing from the sound of forgotten things, a soul hurtling with all its senses, intuition, and disappointments toward joy. Music carries you, buries you, wounds you, cleanses you, and flings open the windows of your memories, childhood, and nostalgia. It doesn't matter if, as a child, you loved the sound of oud strings in the songs of Mehad Hamad or Ali bin Rogha, humming them to yourself by valleys, streams, or mountains, or under the shade of palm trees; or if you used to listen to Mozart, Beethoven, or Bach on the balcony of your apartment in any of the world's capitals. For music is music, descended from one pure lineage, one race, one wondrous source. It knows neither racism nor bondage. It's the daughter of beauty, and the mother of freedom and wonder, flying wingless to distant horizons, breaking through the boundaries of place, language, and ideology, falling over thresholds, hills, and memories without injuring itself, without its blood curdling or its branches drying up.

s

Unbroken and ceaseless, music is what ties people to the memory of land, blood, war, birth, tears, and laughter. It's the creaking of a child's cradle and the crutch of old age that leads to serene springs. It's a conjunction in spoken Arabic, but also the root of language and its branches. My friend, don't look for music in the markets, for it's too pure to be bought or sold. You have to only listen to the breeze blowing through the branches of a tree in the courtyard of your house, or open the windows of your soul to water bubbling in brooks, or close your eyes and listen to a dove cooing on the outskirts of a village to announce the start of summer. Or imagine a mountain shepherdess's voice leading her flock and the sweet sound of a reed flute. Hear the steps of a woman rushing to an appointment she has eagerly awaited for long years. Her footfalls will prompt you: What is music?

Music is a tear on a forgotten rock in the mountains, or a drop of water carried by a bird flying swiftly to its nest, or the sound of a window swinging shut in an ancient mud house.

s

Sometimes, music is a deadly arrow in the heart of time, life, and ideology that forbids joy, burying it or hanging it on the gallows of illusion, or else it's a knife that banishes the darkness of speech. Music is a seedling that we plant and water with joy, or occasionally with sorrow, so one day we can reap and scatter it like roses upon the train of time hurtling toward war and death. Perhaps it will dissolve the hatred in the hearts of generals and soldiers so that they return to their wives and children. Perhaps they'll abandon their bloodlust for a day, just one day, and not commit the crime of Cain, remembering instead the thresholds of their cozy homes and the songs of their wives.

s

I fear that conversation about music goes on and on without ever getting close to it. Music escapes the prison of speech and writing to penetrate the expanse and the heart. I see it now, surrounded by lovers, friends, and enemies as it passes into the distance, like a cloud carrying thunder, rain, disaster, and the voices of martyrs. I see a street cleaner from Kerala walking around Ruwi listening to the music of his country. I see a woman at the foot of a mountain overlooking Phewa Lake, carrying water, wine, and music down the temple road. I see her sitting on a café's doorstep, making drinks and Buddhist charms for temple-goers and tourists fed up with Europe's streets and its murderous modernity. I see dreamers disguising their dreams with music, revolutionaries igniting their revolution with music, exiles carrying music with the soil of their homelands. I see generals bringing music to fateful battles, using it to inflame the lust for blood in the hearts and dreams of their soldiers.

s

Caravan of old age's anxieties, music leads us to the tree we left to die because of drought and our sins. Music worries about itself as it coaches the Sufi's finger or the dancer's foot. It wounds and is wounded, it *is* the wound, it's blood and tears, and it is also the scent of a lover's presence or absence.

Dear music, everyone loves your fruits, sorrows, blood, nostalgia, madness, and purity. Everyone tries to scatter you on his soil: general, prisoner, dancer, shepherd, poet, traveler, the dead, the exiled, the murderer, and the murdered. Everyone turns to you and returns wounded or heartbroken. You collector of contradictions, stealer of light, inspirer of lovers' dreams: please be kind to the tears of the weary.

s

Are you standing or sitting? It doesn't matter, for what's important is that, in the end, music raises your spirits to the heights of wonder or plumbs the depths of your pain. It perches on the balcony, watching its enemies and madmen roam the streets at night. A poet will tell you that music ends with a thousand notes because it lifts us up to its worlds and its wounds. The grammarian will write music below the line so its voice doesn't escape, but it'll surprise him in his sleep, shattering his rigid rules and soaring up from the window toward the expanse flush with metaphor.

Music has the capacity to drag us down to the depths of its astonishment and up to the hills of its desire, penetrating the soul's furthest reaches to awaken within us memories, tears, joys, and disappointments. It can abduct us from reality and transport us into its aesthetic realm, exhume our longings, and make lovers weep. On balconies and in alleyways, music will remain eternal, uniting poor and affluent alike in its love.

The Blood of Solitude

1

Writing is the most thankless of acts, utterly, terrifyingly thankless, stealing time, solitude, age, and ideas, giving us nothing in return but fatigue and alienation.

At home, on the road, in the morning, at the café, in my child's laughter, in the thirst of the trees by my house, in the absence of friends, in the embers of nostalgia or the desolation of loss, writing is my master. Yet, though I'm weary and despondent, it is my last refuge.

2

I dream about writing that offers insights, looks for the shadows of animate and inanimate objects, and goes into the depth of details, unapologetically biased toward the marginal. I look for writing that flows from pain.

I write because writing is the voice that expresses my being in this fleeting, deceptive, and illusory life. I write to catch an ephemeral thought in the morning, or in a story, or in childhood. I write because writing springs from eternal beauty, sailing through oblivion, marginalization, and darkness.

I write to make the pain that tears our souls more beautiful and less painful.

Writing was like a spring for the first man, the one who drew his fear on cave walls. His drawings turned into words that tilled the earth and hunted strange beasts. That first man's drawings tumbled down from cave walls and sprouted wings, then turned into poems that flew up to the skies of language.

Writing is action, not reaction. It's a wound, not blood. It springs from human light, never from ugly or hateful desire. At its deepest, writing is resistance to marginalization, not a search for light.

I write to make the voices of mountain shepherds more tender in spirit. I write to cleanse the woman headed for the spring, toward death and loss, to soothe her with words and tears.

3

Solitude and writing are the blood and voice of one being. They are the music of the soul to which only a few listen. Solitude is a woman walking languidly to the desert, whom I pursue like a blind man following his foresight. Writing is a clear stream from which I drink so that the killers of life, beauty, and peace can't assassinate me.

Writing is a field we till every morning with dreams, words, and ideas, while solitude is the rain that makes the field bloom after a time or after a lifetime.

All glory to writing and to solitude!

4

Write about your solitude, the solitude of the tree in the forest, the loneliness of the stream in the mountains, the sadness of the poet in the poem. Write about the solitude of writing, noble, pure solitude that swaddles the soul in silence. Solitude teaches your heart that light incinerates butterflies and massacres knowledge. Only shadows perceive the true nature of things and their aesthetic essence.

So don't follow the sun of the generals or the lights of illusion. Like a Sufi, you must listen to what the shadows say. Watch the child's wonder in a mirror, contemplate the waitress's sadness at a café or in a poem. Be like a blind man leading the flock of his stories in the mirrors of time.

5

Writing that eludes me, fleeing like a mountain goat from the cage of paper and screen; writing that burrows behind thresholds, that emerges from the depths of simple thoughts; writing that is concealed or revealed by language, or flows from the margins or shadows; writing that probes the depths of pain and joy; writing that is dream, reality, and imagination, that captures present and future moments; writing that tortures me like a blind executioner or amazes me like a child's laughter; writing that binds me to an idea as if I were a criminal in a courtroom; writing that is the root and the tree, the shadow and the silhouette, the shepherd and the reed flute: that's the writing I think of, always.

6

Pain will speak about the solitude of speech, of mountain streams and trees, of the poet, the prisoner, and the shepherd. At night a blind bird will sing about the shadows of solitude searching for a missing Sufi. The blind bird's song will raise a dead child from his grave and lead him to distant mountain springs, where he'll sleep under a lonely tree. As he slumbers, the tree will ask, "What does an orphan do with an absent woman's music?"

Acknowledgments

Notes

Acknowledgments

The author extends thanks and appreciation to his translator, Zia Ahmed, and editor, Laura Fish.

Sara Khalili graciously gave permission to reprint her translation from the Farsi of "Ode to a Tree" by Siavash Kasrai.

"Music" and "The Blood of Solitude" first appeared in *Asymptote* under the title "On Music, Writing and Solitude."

Notes

The Raven of Ruwi

1. Salalah is Oman's third-largest city, one of the largest ports on the Arabian Peninsula.—Trans.

2. Abdullah Habib is an Omani writer and filmmaker.

3. A *falaj* is an ancient water channel. Several of Oman's irrigation systems are on the UNESCO list of World Heritage Sites.—Trans.

4. *Karak* is black tea with milk (preferably evaporated), sugar, and spices—cardamom, cinnamon, cloves, sometimes ginger or saffron—simmered to sublimeness, sold in humble cafés across Oman. The ubiquity of Indian-Pakistani masala chai—*karak* is Urdu for strong or stiff—is surprising in coffee-drinking Arab culture until one recalls that the Persian Gulf states run on South Asian labor.—Trans.

5. Imam Azzan bin Qais (d. 1871) declared a short-lived imamate before he was killed in Mutrah.

The White Goat's Head

1. Sheikh Saeed bin Khalfan bin Ahmed al-Khalili (1811–71) was a religiopolitical figure in the state of Imam Azzan bin Qais. He made several attempts to restore the imamate in the nineteenth century.

2. Ali al-Maamari (1958–2013) was one of Oman's most prominent literary figures.—Trans.

The Storybird Eats the Fish of Mutrah

1. Sir Wilfred Patrick Thesiger (1910–2003), also known as Mubarak bin London (the blessed one of London), was a British military officer, explorer, and writer. He led two camel expeditions across the Empty Quarter and traveled in inner Oman.—Trans.

The Guardian of Muscat

1. Dr. Wells Thoms (d. 1971), American physician and missionary, lived and worked in Oman for more than three decades.—Trans.

Post Office of the Dead

1. The *gharbī* is a scorching wind that blows during the summer months.

Who Stole Muscat's Noses?

1. The Banyans, a Hindu merchant community, have been settled in Oman for centuries.—Trans.

Trees of Ash

1. Fernando Pessoa, *The Collected Poems of Alberto Caeiro*, trans. Chris Daniels (Bristol: Shearsman Books, 2007), 60.—Trans.

2. Abbas Kiarostami (1940–2016) was an Iranian film director, screenwriter, poet, and photographer.—Trans.

3. In Islamic theology, the Sidrat al-Muntahā (lit. "Lote Tree of the Farthest Boundary") is a large lote tree that marks the utmost boundary in the seventh heaven, where the knowledge of the angels ends.—Trans.

4. The *'al'alān* is a perennial tree under threat of extinction. Spread over Oman's mountain ranges, it has therapeutic properties and a pleasant aromatic scent.

5. The *'itma* is a small evergreen tree. The stem is sinuous, profusely branched. It grows in the Jabal Akhdar (Green Mountain) range and the highlands of Oman's Dhofar governorate.

6. Siavash Kasrai, *Selected Poems: As Red as Fire, Tasting of Smoke*, trans. Sara Khalili (Tehran: Sokhan, 2007), 137. Siavash Kasrai (1927–96) was a noted Iranian poet and political activist.—Trans.

Hamoud Saud is an Omani writer of short stories and literary nonfiction. His writing frequently appears in Arabic newspapers and culture magazines, and some of it has been translated into Azerbaijani, English, Japanese, and Spanish. Among his published works are *The Military Turban* (2013), *The Woman Returning from the Forest Sings* (2015), *The Bank Raven and the Scent of Ruwi* (2017), *Dreams Suspended on Wadi Adai Bridge* (2019), and *Trees of Ash and the Blind Man of Marrakesh* (2022).

Zia Ahmed's translations of Arabic fiction and literary nonfiction have appeared in *Asymptote*, *Denver Quarterly*, and the *Markaz Review*. He lived in Oman for three years before returning to Virginia.